Kirsten Hunter is an Australian author and psychologist whose crime fiction series combines psychology, suspense, and characters that you can relate to; you love them, or you love to hate them. She is the bestselling author of adult and child psychology books, but her true passion is psychological puzzle mysteries. Kirsten lives in Toowoomba with her husband Jon and their five boys.

Kirstenhunterauthor.com

Or follow Kirsten on

Facebook @KirstenHunterAuthor
Instagram @KirstenHunterAuthor

MURDER

AT THE NARCISSUS

GARDENING CLUB

By Kirsten Hunter

First published 2023 by Kirsten Hunter

Produced by Independent Ink
independentink.com.au

Cover design by Zach Lawry
Edited by Samantha Sainsbury and Jane Smith
Internal design by Independent Ink
Typeset in 12/16 pt Minion Pro by Post Pre-press Group, Brisbane

ISBN 978-1-922742-28-5 (paperback)
ISBN 978-1-922742-29-2 (epub)
ISBN 978-1-922742-30-8 (kindle)

PROLOGUE

YOUR LIFE CAN CHANGE in one night; your life is taken, your life begins, you take a life. This is what Anna discovered on this fateful night at the Narcissus Gardening Club, a club supposedly named after the daffodil, not the members.

CHAPTER I

I FOUND MYSELF IN the garden that night with the person that I disliked perhaps the most in the world, my husband.

'You could either laugh or cry.' I said. 'But your not capable of either.' I'd never normally be this bold with Niles, but for this one moment, I felt brave, drunk brave, drunk on exhaustion. Tonight could've been special, I'd really been looking forward to it, but instead I was here with him. The stone in my shoe that had become a boulder.

Niles stared at me. At his wife. He shot me a warning glance. 'What are you talking about?' he said. 'Why are you being like this?'

'Like what?'

'Just not like *you*.'

'Not the doormat you're used to?' Niles gave me a mocking scowl. I had spoken a truth that we both knew to be fact. But he knew and I knew that he would never admit it. Something within me had cracked. This place might only have been just a garden to some people, for me, however, it was more; it was my escape. And tonight somehow the person who hurt me the most had made it into the inner walls of my sanctuary. The troll had made it into the secret garden. This was the last straw.

Niles and I stood in silence. There was nothing more to say. I spun on my heel; I searched for something to look at, something to take me back to my surrounds. I needed to get out of my head. The sun dangled on the horizon; it was in no hurry. At a distance, the large, shady trees that surrounded the garden's perimeter cast long shadows that didn't seem to end. Their heavy silhouettes simply laced together with the darkness.

The garden beds to our left were where I spend most of my time at this gardening club, The Narcissus Gardening Club. I'd won this allocated garden bed as a random prize, a draw that I was sure a dear friend had entered me into, and on arriving to the club I came to realise that I was the envy of many of the long-term gardeners. My plot was close to the garden sheds and the watering hose, so apparently I was a bit of a garden tramp. I wondered if these twenty raised garden beds meant that there were twenty garden-club members. I'd never worked that out.

'No, we shouldn't break up; we shouldn't separate!' This is what Niles had said tonight when I'd told him for the umpteenth time that I wanted a divorce. The irony was that I'd just explained that he didn't listen to me. That he didn't see me. That I was invisible to him. I wasn't actually in the relationship; I was just a body double of a wife. And here he was saying that he didn't agree that we should breakup, like it was some sort of democracy. I wasn't allowed to not want to be with him anymore. I'd just responded in silence. The next thing I knew, he'd invited himself to my garden-club gathering tonight. He just got in the car with me. And here we were. Why he could possibly want to be here I had no idea. He had only ever had scorn for my gardening-club involvement. So much so that I often wondered if coming along was worthwhile given Niles' carry-on when I'd get home.

I studied the crisply cut grass and the determined patches of wild daisies. He stood too close to me. My body clenched, a familiar feeling. I just wanted to run. My legs started to walk me away from him. Like magnetic poles, I was simply repelled by him. He clearly felt the opposite. He followed me. This dusky garden was taking on a different personality from its daytime sunshine; I strolled along one of the many pebble paths that led off in different directions. Tonight could've been enchanting.

'What's got into you?' His voice was short.

Shrill laughter suddenly welled up in me. My nervous energy seemed to surprise and confuse Niles as well as me. He frowned again and looked at me like I was some sort of mad person. It was a look I was familiar with, sort of incredulous, as if he was embarrassed for me.

No man's land. I was just coping.

'Really, Anna, I don't know what's got into you. I barely recognise you,' he said.

I was one thread away from the absolute decision to leave him. Not the decision in truth, it was actually about finding enough courage. I had mentally left the building, and he could feel it. I was not falling in line with him anymore. He had lost his power. He looked at me, gloomy, feeling sorry for himself. I was sure he was convinced that he was poorly done by in all of this; a poor me act. I'd come to realise that sometimes he was just working to manipulate me, other times he truly believed his level of entitlement. Unfortunately, he played these two faces with such ease, with such conviction, and I could never tell them apart. Tonight, I didn't care. From now on, I wouldn't care.

During our silent car drive in, it had occurred to me that tonight, again, sleep would elude me. Tonight's anxious restlessness couldn't end in sleep.

I heard the crack of Niles' knuckles as he walked a pace behind me, while the wind seemed to hush him through the trees. The hum of traffic from the suburban streets that surrounded the garden oasis created a subtle grey noise. This community garden was the largest and most impressive in the larger city of Brisbane. Distinct from the noise of cars driving home, a car could be heard intentionally approaching. It was getting closer, the gravel gritting with more intensity now. It would soon park, the second lot of guests were to arrive at this community affair. While this was a relief to me, I felt a wave of anxiety, of anticipation.

'So, what's the dress code for this thing tonight?' His tone was almost civilised. I waited to hear his true agenda. 'I mean, they're probably going to come in their gardening gear right? Their rags, like you … really Anna … you should put some energy in. Take some pride.' And there it was.

'Niles, why are you here?'

He didn't skip a beat. 'I thought we could have some time together? Some couple time, like the counsellor suggested.'

I felt a punch to my stomach; how could he completely ignore where I was at, the state of our relationship? The curtain was closing, closed. I was solemn in my reply, 'You mean when she suggested that two years ago, when it wasn't your priority? When you cancelled the second session without even asking me. Honestly Niles, I don't know why you're here.'

Niles seemed to make a contorted effort to lighten the topic. 'Better late than never.'

'You think?' I just eyeballed him as I changed direction to take a path toward our meeting place.

'What's that noise?' Niles seemed alarmed by something he couldn't place. 'It sounds like a creature growling?'

I was amused because he was right. 'That's Babcia.'

Niles straightened up; I noticed his shoulders go

back, his chin up, his chest out. He was a male about to parade. Taking aim at me he said, 'So, I'm going to meet the Queen, the Jester, the Princess, the General, Fetch and my favourite, the Goddess?'

'Shush!' I gasped. 'I wouldn't have told you my silly names for them if I *ever* imagined you were actually going to meet them. All those hundreds of times you haven't listened to me, and you've actually listened to this?'

Niles had me very concerned at this point. My worlds were colliding together, and my joking made in the privacy of our home could well become public knowledge, ammunition for him. Niles would take delight in stealing this haven from me. The Narcissus Gardening Club was a threat to him, his opponent. He would use this against me, again isolate me from my people.

'I like these people, be kind to them,' I pleaded stupidly. As I said this, I flinched; I'd just secured his target. My only hope lay in the fact that Niles relied heavily on his charm arsenal in public. His real damage was done behind closed doors.

'You like them?' Niles sounded surprised.

'They're not "go a road trip" kind of people, and they're not "share your world" kind of people, but yeah I like them. They're characters, and they remind me to laugh. I need that.'

The absurdity of the characters at the Narcissus Gardening Club was quite delicious to me, but I wouldn't share this with Niles. I wouldn't put more gun powder in his artillery.

*

Actually, two cars had arrived. Tabitha pulled up at the same time as Babcia and Remy. I saw a slender leg, stockinged, complete with two-inch leopard-print heels, emerge from the open door. Then the rest of her appeared, clad as usual in a figure-hugging leopard-print dress. From this distance, I had to admit, she looked in pretty good shape for a sixty-two-year-old. Her hands were the only part of her that betrayed the truth of her age as her skin had that paper delicacy. But her hands were also strangely red; they looked somehow punished. She glanced our way; she looked Niles up and down, fluttering her eyelash extensions. She had no shame. She patted her bottle-brown hair and sashayed, hips swaying for Niles's benefit, toward Babcia's car.

I was sure that Tabitha thought that she was the main prize for any man she met. Regarding this deluded world of hers, I always thought, *good on you*. I figured that she wasn't doing too much harm and she seemed to be having a wonderful time in her own world.

My favourite game was, 'how shall Tabitha be wearing leopard print today?' Tonight she had outdone herself. Even when she was up to her elbows in dirt, working on her garden bed, Tabitha was guaranteed to be wearing animal print in some form, and, of course, she'd be wearing her elegant brooch. She never seemed to leave home without it. A creature of habit perhaps. Tabitha was the sort who would never, in time, concede to being old. That would be undignified.

Tabitha swanned over to the second car. She beelined for Remy as he got out of the driver's seat. I saw his eyes flicker in her direction, but he just turned and walked with purpose around to Babcia's car door. As she emerged, Babcia released a throaty scoff reserved for Tabitha. Babcia had been sitting with her car window down, taking in all of her surrounds. This, I now realise, was how Niles first heard her strange, throaty noise moments ago, her famous call to the wild. She growled from such depth and with such authority that I was sure she always meant something offensive.

Tabatha seemed determined to ignore Babcia's reproach; she just pushed on and followed after Remy, hands on her waist, gyrating hips protruding to each side. She stood beside Remy, though he refused to meet her eyes. She leaned in for a presumptuous hello kiss. He awkwardly complied. A bit like a trapped animal really. Not one cheek, but a sequence of three. Poor Remy, he looked mildly flustered to be drawn into this facade.

'Don't mind me.' Tabitha fluttered her eyelashes at him. 'It's my European heritage. My family always kiss three times.'

Babcia barked, 'That is putrid truth, how come you're only European with Remy? You are a hussy, nothing more; you would flirt with a scarecrow if it was standing! You have no shame!'

Tabitha ignored Babcia and, as she turned toward the path, I saw that my prediction was right: Tabitha was wearing the brooch. It was a delicate little lily, quite pretty. I had always wanted to ask her if it was a family heirloom. For her to wear it religiously it must have had sentimental value. But it was my rule not to talk to Tabitha. I could watch and enjoy her from a distance. I had enough genuine stress in my life. I wasn't about to engage with someone who embodied drama.

'Remy, darling, could you help carry my basket?' asked Tabitha in her best feminine voice. Remy silently slung his fold up chair over his shoulder, picked up Tabitha's basket, and then returned with his other arm interlinked with Babcia to assist her to our banquet area.

Niles and I stood at the entrance to their path as if we were receiving them to the gardens. Remy's glance danced from Niles to me. His smile softened as it rested on me. Babcia simply stared at Niles. I felt him stiffen next to me, but he smiled and extended his hand. 'So glad to meet you and to see this beautiful garden at last,' he said. 'Anna has told me so much about it.'

Babcia grunted and ignored Niles' outstretched hand, but Remy took it and smiled warmly. 'Welcome,' he said.

We stepped aside as this procession walked past us.

We were apparently not in Tabitha's line of vision. As she continued to pursue poor Remy, she gushed, 'Isn't it lovely that we're all here together on this beautiful evening, Remy?'

With effort, Babcia stopped and pivoted to face Tabitha, and in a tone that made Niles pull up sharply beside me, she growled loudly, 'Fe, do not praise the day before sunset!'

Tabitha gasped and recoiled. Despite her hurt school-girl face, I could see she was enjoying the drama of this injury. She then straightened her dress and shuffled to resume walking slightly to the side of Babcia and Remy. Tabitha would never defer to walk behind others.

I was content to watch the trio from a distance. To watch the circus unfold. Remy stood with strength at Babcia's side. I believe Babcia could've walked without Remy's support, but it warmed my heart to see how he was making it easier for her. Remy was one of those men who looked as attractive from behind as from in front. I'd had many opportunities to notice. Always at Babcia's side, Remy was someone I hoped to see on my arrival each time I would come to the gardening club. I'd find myself looking for him, scanning for him. He has such an easy way about him, so relaxed, so under-stated. Remy somehow looked strangely stylish in his carelessly casual clothes. I had the impression that he didn't own a lot of clothes, but that each piece was quality, cared for and worn with time.

'So here we have, can I guess … the Queen, *clearly* Princess, and who's the guy, Anna?' asked Niles, waking me up from my private thoughts.

'That's Remy and Babcia, and that's Tabitha.'

'Yeah, but who's the guy?' I really didn't know how to tackle this. If I avoided these explanations completely, then he'd just persist throughout the evening. Niles looked intent in thought for a moment. 'Fetch, I'm guessing he's Fetch?' Niles laughed. He only seemed to laugh when he was laughing at someone else's expense. 'That's a bit mean, Anna!'

*

The garden grounds were clearly laid out by an ambitious hand. The open, expansive area to the south was checkered with our raised garden beds all standing to neat attention. They were a piece of work in themselves. Thick recycled timber, each with their own story, their own past. Nestled as a viewing place for the gardening efforts was a rest area, affectionately called The Hub. While this was the favourite resting place to sit and recover from your labour, it was more importantly a place to chat with gardening neighbours. Someone had even brought in a bar fridge. It was covered of course with a ratty blanket. We couldn't advertise our prized drinks to random people who might wander in at night. Scattered timber garden sheds were aplenty, with communal tools laying around or neatly hung up. This generous area then funnelled into a long arbour lined with camellias on either side. The arbour stretched for such a distance that you couldn't see its destination. It had become a bit wild and chaotic as it had taken on various climbing plants over the years all interwoven: roses, potato vine and jasmine amongst them. The aromas along the arbour some how filled me with more joy than the visual feast that lay before me.

Halfway along the arbour were openings to the left and to the right. To the right was the nuttery, hosting a variety of nut trees apparently collected over many years. Some small, some tall and some broad. They all intermingled but with enough strategic spacing for the sun to reach their canopy. It was a joy to walk through the nuttery and recognise each of their offerings. The arbour archway to the left took you to the citrus orchard. The members could pick this produce to their heart's content. A large avocado tree drew your attention in the far distance. The messy fruit on the ground and the wild combination of citrus smells made this a whimsical place.

The arbour path then continued to meander forward, revealing at its end the beautiful, rotund, generous Birch Circle, a large, open-air central circle with birch trees dancing around it. This was a meeting place where clearly the original garden designer had decided to relent and allow an expanse of non-productive plants to form their mood. The birch trees created a delicate stirring, a cascade of wind rippled through each layer of trees as they circled out from this communal space. There were several paths leading to this meeting point, as you could approach the garden from several neighbouring streets.

These approaching paths were playfully wild, making the arrival at the Birch Circle an enjoyable unveiling. You would walk through a living tunnel and be greeted by nature's grand pantheon. We arrived to be greeted by two large, square, hardwood tables that took pride of place in this green manor. The barbeque that usually lived at The Hub had already been moved here. Surely Remy had strong-armed it here at an earlier time. On arrival in this circular area, Remy had turned on the freestanding lights that glowed with a soft warmth. They reminded me of old-fashioned streetlights. The aged birch trees now created lovely prancing shadows as the wind gently blew. It was romantic lighting for the strange motley crew that were to gather.

No sooner had we arrived behind them through the arbour, then Babcia barked at Niles, 'You!' I suppressed a smile; Babcia was wasting no time putting him in his place. 'Put my chair here.' She pointed to the position directly between the two tables. Niles jumped to attention. He opened up the substantial camping chair that Remy had momentarily placed down and moved it to where he thought he'd been instructed.

Babcia huffed, 'Tfu.' With harsh, jerking movements,

she moved the chair so that it was placed precisely between the two tables, one table in front of her and the other behind her. She promptly sat down decisively, as if this was the first matter in hand. She'd positioned herself so that the whole party would need to walk either in front or behind her to move through the central area. Her throne was dead centre of the Birch Circle. We would of course all choose to walk behind her; no one would dare enter her personal space and go the front route.

I held back a giggle as Niles actually walked backwards away from Babcia. A peasant deferring to royalty.

'How ridiculous,' Niles growled under his breath, still fixing a smile on his face. And yet there Babcia sat on her throne, and we stood to attention at her mercy. 'Queen, yeah fucking Queen!'

Niles was frothing. It was usual for Babcia to sit on her throne and barely move from it. From her perched position, she'd then throw orders at people, supervise and impose her corrections on their errors. She was even known to get a stick and jab people with it as she directed them. To my relief, there was no stick in reach tonight.

I was about to introduce everyone to Niles, a case of just getting it over with, when I was saved by the entrance of a tall, lanky man. He arrived from a pathway on the far side of the Birch Circle.

'Hello everyone,' said this new person.

Eyes turned to him with surprise. 'I'm William', He hesitated. 'Thanks for having me along.'

There was no reply. He continued, 'I've just joined up so I thought I'd invite myself to this gathering … if that's alright?' Despite his clear nervousness, he had a warm voice. His business pants were well ironed, and his shirt tucked in neatly. My guess was that he normally wore a tie. His smile was broad and open, and his eyes lingered on each of us questioningly.

Tabitha and I automatically shot a look at Babcia. Babcia wouldn't usually stand for this imposition. A stranger, presuming to come to the inner circle of the Narcissus Gardening Club, her precious club, and not even a committee member? I'd taken a deep breath, wishing for the stranger not to have to go through the grilling that seemed inevitable. An outsider couldn't possibly anticipate how formidable this old lady could be. Not just on a bad day, but every day. To my astonishment, Babcia just motioned with her hand. 'Mhm,' was all that came from her mouth.

Happy to extend the reprieve, I stepped forward. I felt a rushed desire to greet this foolhardy stranger with particular warmth. 'Hi William, I'm Anna, and this is Niles.' I had deliberately avoided introducing Niles as my husband. I knew he would chew and growl about this for hours when we got home. I had just given him fodder. Nevertheless, I repeated the omission as I introduced Niles to the other members so far present.

I felt Niles' eyes on me as Babcia and Remy now took the time for a warm hello. 'It was such a great idea to have our gathering at night,' I said, ignoring Niles. 'I've never been here under the stars. It's pretty magical … the garden at night.' Babcia smiled on receiving my hello peck on her cheek. Since we'd met, Babcia had been strangely warm toward me, always reaching for this affection during our greetings and goodbyes. I'd normally give Remy the same peck, but tonight I was guarded. I felt Niles staring into my back. I did this with other friends as well. I shut down when Niles was with me; I had to.

It was so strange to have my new friends and my husband in one place. It was like two parts of me, the carefree part and the emotionally strangled part trying to coexist in the same space, at the same time. The contortions in my stomach tightened. These gardens had strangely been where I've felt safe, in contrast to home. I'd been working to find words to explain what happened at home. At home, when I'd come to Niles with an issue, he'd flip it or twist it, he'd railroad me with half-truths at such speed that I couldn't call him on it. Niles would always have to win the conversation.

It wasn't until I finally spoke to someone that I woke up to all of this. I'd kept the storm of my home life to myself for many years. I'd felt embarrassed. I'd compensate for him, making it all look okay to my friends. I was always making excuses for him.

There was a point where I started journaling, venting, vomiting out my internal world, my internal dialogue, my protests, my confusion, my resolutions, my grief; there was nothing legible in it. I'd just write and write, through my sobbing until there was nothing left. At first, I was terrified of Niles finding my notes, but then I changed. I started to want him to know, to read about the reality of my world.

It was on one especially desperate night, when I was trying yet again to tell him how miserable I was with how he treated me, that I actually went and dropped these journals onto our bed. I said, 'It's all here; this is my pain.' He just scoffed. The journals just sat there unread, discarded, just like me. That was the moment that it truly sunk in. He didn't care. He didn't care about me. I realised that I'd always assumed that because of our history, because we were in a relationship, because we were married, because we had children together, and because I cared for him, that it meant he cared for me. This was when I stepped back and actually looked at his behaviour, and what I saw was his complete disregard for my needs, my pleas, my begging for care. He actually felt nothing for me.

This was an extraordinary moment. I seemed to snap into another reality. I started to look at him through completely different eyes. I started to *truly* look at him.

I started to see how it made absolutely no difference how incredibly cautious and diplomatic I approached an issue; he would be unreasonable and often erupt. I saw his patterns: how he'd minimise and manipulate, how he'd attack the people and the things that I loved. I realised this was his toolbox; this was his arsenal. I began to step back. He was not my love anymore. I was not looking to him to be loved, to be understood, or for my needs to be met. This gave me power. I was no longer in the position to be disappointed and be hurt, as I no longer expected anything from him. He was so predictable.

Then the strangest thing happened. He became ridiculous to me.

During my visits to my garden oasis, I'd become increasingly intrigued to find out about Remy's back-story. With Babcia always holding court, however, it had never felt comfortable to chat on this level while we were gardening. This mind you, didn't stop Babcia asking about my personal world. She loved to hear about my kids and my mundane, daily carry-on. I didn't talk about Niles though, which I was sure was a tell for her. She was a very switched-on woman.

This was when it happened. This was when the ship hit the ice. I was taken from my thoughts back to the world around me, to the awareness that Niles was actually talking to Babcia. Why he had approached her was lost on me. In light of her earlier slam down, he'd usually decide she was an arsehole and not waste his charm on her. That was his word for almost everyone: arsehole. But here he was, clearly trying to make conversation?

He gingerly said, 'I see that you have a Russian accent. I think it's great when people keep their accents.'

Babcia almost had a fit. 'I am Polish!' she barked indignantly. 'Russia and Poland are not even from the same Slavic group. You, young man, know nothing of what you speak!'

Niles looked to me to be rescued. 'Yes of course, I'm so sorry … sorry to offend.'

Tabitha, however, was happy to interject here, to divert Niles from the snap of Babcia's jaws. She was of course launching into her usual show for Niles. A man. A new man in the group. She smiled at him coyly and staged an elegant wander toward him. As an aside, she glanced to me and said, 'Anna, you must be loving having your man along to our little soirée!'

'Yeah,' I replied with a deadpan voice. 'I'm super jazzed!'

Tabitha missed my sarcasm and smiled warmly at Niles. She looked into his eyes as if they had some intimacy between them. I didn't feel uncomfortable about this at all, not a drop. *Have him,* was my thought.

'Lovely to meet you. Tabitha, was it?' Niles crooned. 'You don't look like you do much gardening.'

'Oh,' she fluttered, 'a girl should always make some effort.' She placed her hand on the curve of her hip, her Tabitha pose.

Tabitha was on a roll, and, noticing that Babcia and Remy had not gone on to engage with William, she swiftly turned from Niles to the other new man in the group. Sidling up to him, she placed a manicured hand on his arm and spoke so softly to him that he had to bend close to her ear. Never mind that he was young enough to be her son, or that there was a wedding band on his finger. There was a general sigh amongst the group as we watched her cast her temptress magic. *Try*, that is. The poor man was fresh meat.

*

Along another of the paths, steps could be heard on the stones and gravel. As the sun was melting almost completely from the sky, everything was taking on more of a hidden presence, every entrance held intrigue. Jacob stepped through this wall of green. Jacob was, as usual, all smiles and wearing his farmer's flat cap and dated spectacles. Jacob, I believed, would've thought that he looked very smart.

'Hello everyone, I'm here,' he said. He rocked as he walked. 'The party can begin now.' There was a chuckle through the group, though I'm sure his intention was to impress, not to provide comic relief. Jacob was literal and therefore pretty absurd. He collided so often with social etiquette and remained oblivious as he pranced along, his confidence and seeming superiority a result of his sheer ignorance.

Jacob welcomed the group into his presence, as if acknowledging individuals at an assembly. He was met with a general nodding of heads and subtle raising of eyebrows. There was, however, no particular warmth toward him or extension of conversation. This, of course, didn't deter him. I didn't think he even noticed. 'Well, are you all organised for the party then? No one drop the ball and arrive a freeloader?'

After all of his sixty or seventy years of life, I always wondered how could an adequately intelligent person like Jacob still be so utterly oblivious of his own rudeness? He spoke with a sharpness of tongue. Was he malicious – or just a fool? A bumbling fool, most likely, a jester, ignorant of the damage that he created at full throttle. He seemed happy enough, however, in his misguided belief that people were fortunate to have his charming company.

Jacob registered the two new additions to the group in the form of William and Niles. 'You're a tall one,' Jacob said unhelpfully waving his hand up and down as if sizing up William. William grimaced. I doubt he knew where to go with this comment. Jacob continued to unashamedly study William. William towered over Jacob, yet Jacob looked at him as if it was the reverse.

Jacob then shuffled beside Niles. Motioning his chin at Babcia, he said to Niles. 'She's from Poland you know. I've heard bad things about the Poles.' I felt a hush roll over the group.

Did Jacob's rudeness have any limit? Standing there, absentmindedly playing with his wedding ring, he *seemed* unaware of the ripples of offence he was causing.

This was my cue. I always stepped away from Jacob's campaigns, and on this occasion, I couldn't afford for the seed of this discussion to sprout. You see, I seemed to get on with Babcia when no one else but Remy did, or, more to the point, Babcia seemed to get on with *me*, and the thought of sabotaging this delicate treaty because of Jacob's ignorant comments made my heart palpitate. I loved being part of this odd, exclusive clique within the Narcissus Club. I felt special. And without it, I wouldn't have had access to Remy. The day that I won the prize of my garden bed and my membership, my life got richer. There was no way that the little ferret Jacob was going to sabotage this.

'We had better start setting up,' I said in an attempt to make an abrupt exit. Niles followed like a lost sheep.

'So you call this one Jester right? He's not funny; he just makes stupid comments,' Niles quietly growled into my ear.

'Are Jesters actually funny,' I said flatly. 'Or just trying to be.'

I was sure that Niles came here thinking that he could infiltrate my safe space, but he was meeting characters that made him spin a little off his axis. I watched him eyeing Babcia warily. He would've hated that he'd been an obedient soldier to her command. He wasn't alone. I'd seen many people backpedal away from her, shocked by her abrupt orders. They'd retreat looking stunned, thoroughly on the back foot. And tonight, Babcia had seemed to set her sights on Niles for some reason. But I had no sympathy for him. My bully was being met with another, larger version of a bully. Was it vindication that I felt? A bit of natural justice perhaps?

I suddenly felt this strange shiver and tension run through my body. My mind had returned from its brief reprieve to the thought that just kept banging away in my head, gnawing at me since we left home. *Why didn't I stop Niles from coming tonight?* I was such an idiot, truly. I should have spoken up. I should have gotten straight out of the car and told him decisively that he wasn't invited, that I wasn't going with him. But no, the idiot that I was, I just sat there frozen, shocked that he got in the car with me in the first place. But in truth, I just didn't have the fight in me. But I really needed tonight. That was my error. I had let him know about my excitement. I therefore knew that his strategy would be to sabotage what was important to me. To rant and rave at some minuscule issue. He knew that tonight was important to me, so he was going to divebomb it for sure. And there we were.

I felt claustrophobic as my two worlds overlapped. It wasn't fair that he was here. This was the space where the mouse could escape the cat, and now the cat had got in.

Niles lived in our home and at his work … his business, our business in truth. That was it; there was no outside world to him. He went to work, came home and disappeared into his beers. I didn't know which person I disliked more, sober Niles or drunk Niles. He had shaped our existence so that there were few outside people in our life. I'd lost so many friends, but fortunately not all, not my life long, true friend Alicia.

It wasn't until I started to wake up from this strange world that I had to admit it. I hated to admit it, but I'd succumbed to his brainwashing, I'd started to think that I was being unreasonable to put my hand up, to voice my needs, to hold him accountable when he'd cut me down and be cruel. He'd hammer me that I was the one who had *made him angry*. The eggshells I was walking on had become normal ground to me.

The day I told Alicia it was not a planned thing. It was more that the dam wall broke. I broke. When I finally shared with her what was happening, her astonishment, her depth of sadness and outrage shook me to my core. I learned that what I was telling her was clearly not okay. My world was not okay. When I opened the curtains of my hidden world to her, the fog in my head began to lift. She told me what I deep down always knew. This was unhealthy. This was not to be tolerated. This had to stop.

And that was where I was that night. I was leaving him. But when? How? I didn't know. In my head I'd left him already, and now I was oscillating all over the place. Shock, relief, fury, deep sadness and fear. Mainly fear. *How do I do this?* Alicia had a solution and begged me to come and live with her so that was the plan. But what about after that? Could I take on Niles? He had always kept me from leaving by saying that he would go after the kids. But he was a stranger to them. Would he carry this through? Just the thought of this had kept me paralysed all these years. And the legal fight. How would I fight when I was a limp version of myself? I had no money behind me, and Niles had left us in a financial mess. I thought I surely couldn't rely on Alicia as much as she insisted I could. I had so much to chew over. And then there was that thought again. *Why didn't I stop him from coming tonight?*

I sensed that Niles could feel the shift in power away from him. That had him holding on even tighter. The noose was edging from around my neck, and he kept trying to lasso the power back. I was watching his attempts with fresh eyes. Tragic laughter really. And there we were. The absurd state of affairs between Niles and I was now joined by the wonderfully absurd gathering of this Narcissus Gardening Club. Sometimes there are moments in life where you truly feel like you must be on a stage.

*

Babcia sat, short and round, upon her throne. She had a low and secure centre of gravity. Somehow she looked all of her eighty-two years and yet radiated vital energy. I could never imagine her having been young; it was as if she'd always been older than her years.

'What's with the grey cardigan; it's an absolute rag,' Niles said into my ear. 'Surely the queen can afford better clothes, no matter how poor she is.'

I ignored him. I actually liked how Babcia always wore her grey cardigan. I'd decided a while ago that she wore it for the convenience of its now-stretched pockets. She'd pull out all sorts of things from those pockets. I think this was her replacement for a handbag. It was endearing. That grey cardigan was her uniform. She'd burrow around for what she needed, a mint, a seed packet, a handkerchief, a small tube of hand cream. While Babcia would dress in her greys and browns, as if she wanted to be in the background, her personality was anything but deferring.

Watching Babcia muttering in Polish as she rummaged, I couldn't help smiling. Looking away so she wouldn't see my amusement, I met Remy's gaze. He grinned at me as he placed a protective hand on Babcia's shoulder.

'Is that what you're after?' he said gently to her as he passed her a packet of her favourite mints. He knew her. He anticipated her.

I'd spent hours imagining the backstory of how these two came into each other's lives. I knew Remy worked for Babcia, but I felt sure he wasn't with her only for the sake of employment; his dedication had to be personal. As for Babcia, who seemed to look down on everyone: she didn't look down on the one person here who she employed. Whatever the bridge was between them, it was a curious and beautiful thing.

Even though I had never been the pedestrian hit by Babcia's prickly onslaught, I still couldn't relax with her. I was sure that her kindness to me somehow had more to do with Remy. Perhaps Babcia had seen that Remy and I were friendly, and she was humouring me for his sake. As for Niles' view of her tonight, I didn't care a bit. Babcia could look after herself.

My thoughts were broken by the sudden arrival of Dean emerging from behind the tool shed that backed on to the Birch Circle. 'Good evening, middle-class suburbians,' he said. I was sure he thought he epitomised clever wit.

Dean looked like a stiff peg walking. Hands clenched together at his front, shoulders held broad, head carried with tension, he looked more like a bouncer than someone attending a gardening club. With his spindly legs, Dean was one of those peculiar types who just worked their upper body. His skivvy of neck muscle was so thick that he could now barely turn his head. I often marveled at this evolutionary fail every time I caught him having to rotate his body to make a sideways glance. This heavy-laden tree of a man with his twiggy trunk had arrived at our little gathering.

Somehow I found myself absent-mindedly talking to Niles. 'What's the difference between misogynistic and sexist?'

'What?'

'A misogynist and a sexist.'

'Huh?' Niles frowned at me.

'I've often wondered about that.'

'Who's this one?' asked Niles.

I replied quietly, 'That's Dean.'

'No, which of your pet names?'

'Leave it.'

Niles looked into the distance. I heard him recount, 'The Queen is Babcia, the Princess is Tabitha, Jacob is the Jester … Fetch is him …' His eyes widened. 'The General.' He smiled at me, his smile broadened further when he saw my awkwardness. 'Anna, you've nailed it. Your names, your pet names … they match perfectly. So … Dean is the General, hey? Yep!'

'I exhaled, 'I was being sarcastic.'

'Yes, I can see it; he's a lot, isn't he,' Niles said.

'You all having riveting chatter? Gratuitous travelogue for the cafe society,' Dean said.

'What is he saying? This guy's amazing.' Niles had at least brought his hand to his face to hide his broad grin.

'I never know,' I said. A rare moment we were in agreement.

Dean had now singled Tabitha out. 'I'm sure you've

all been chatting away, all Garp-like caricature and hyperbole.'

I'm sure that Dean didn't know what he was saying half the time. He often made little sense. It was obvious that he would collect what to him was impressive language and fling it out at his first opportunity. At every opportunity.

Dean wore black pants, a white business shirt and black dress shoes. He always wore this ensemble to the gardening club committee meetings and looked very out of place. I never saw him actually tend a garden plot. Come to think of it I'd only seen Jacob garden on the rare occasion too. Why Dean would wear this penguin outfit so proudly was lost on me. He always looked like he'd come from a funeral.

I wanted to wander around and extract myself from Niles. A difficult thing as Niles wouldn't detach and mingle. I was drowning in his unwanted company.

We were now a party of eight. I watched Babcia glancing at Niles, Dean and Jacob. In turn, these three were also sizing each other up from their separate corners with not-so-subtle glances at each other. They were scanning each other and not bothering to mask their interest. For some reason, they weren't paying William any attention. Perhaps they thought he was a one-off ring-in who would leave as soon as he'd just come.

'The scythe met the stone,' Babcia scoffed as she watched the trio of men. She ran her gnarled hand along her short, straight, grey bob. Her harsh hair line accentuated her round face, round nose and round cheeks. One day over a garden bed, I'd ventured to Remy that these bizarre riddles of hers were her 'Babciaisms'. How Babcia didn't run out of her eccentric sayings amazed me. Given any opportunity, she'd whirl up and spit one straight in your eye.

This was the 'settling-in' stage, something I enjoyed watching whenever I went to gatherings. Everyone sniffing each other on their arrival. We weren't much above dogs, just a bit more discreet perhaps. Those with fragile egos trying to soothe their own sense of inadequacy by looking down on others.

William made an effort to make conversation with Babcia. 'Are you happy with the numbers?'

'Every stick has two ends,' she said, her beady eyes piercing him with unapologetic intensity.

Remy and I looked at each other for translation, but clearly he, as usual, was just as puzzled as I was. As we had done so many times before, we stood confused, pretending to understand Babcia. But William just smiled.

Babcia, now speaking plainly, said, 'People, I don't like them, but we need people to have a party, and the Narcissus Gardening Club deserves a party.'

The moment of awkward silence continued. A group of people, like slightly frayed pieces of a jigsaw puzzle that just don't fit together.

*

'Where is she? Where is that infernal woman?' The tranquillity of the garden was again jarred by Babcia's barking words.

With a general look of confusion, everyone started to look around searching for this *infernal woman* to emerge from the many green avenues.

Meanwhile, Tabitha cocked her head at Babcia and said with great self-importance, 'I can't stay long this evening, Babcia. I have a prior engagement.'

Babcia gripped on to the arms of her chair, her knuckles white under her paper-thin skin. In her thick Polish accent she said, 'She who wants to leave, stick a nail in her foot.' If you couldn't understand her through her accent, it was your problem. It would never have been Babcia's intention to assimilate.

Tabitha recoiled and moved to the back of the group discreetly. I wouldn't have known what to do with those words either.

As if waiting for an entrance, my favourite person, Margot Gray, breezed in from along the scented arbour.

'Well hello lovelies! Looking forward to your delicious company tonight. Apparently, we're both throwing a party and we're the guests.' Margot smiled broadly, her tone was her usual, warm and welcoming. Her eyes danced around the leafy room until they rested on William. The boldness of her smile astounded me. She contorted her face playfully. Was she flirting with William? No, that wasn't it. I couldn't place it. It was like she was rushing to him while she stood still. There was a lightness in her toward him, even more than usual. A broad, quizzical grin danced on her lips and through her eyes. Maybe he was her love interest. My mind spun as I tried to place what I was seeing. No, it wasn't sexual. I ended up with this conclusion at least. Then what was it?

Babcia again grabbed the side of her chair with firm hands and twisted to her left to firmly eyeball Margot. 'You're late! I said six pm! I told you that that is when we were starting; I have a right to be listened to. You have no respect.' Her voice came from deep in her throat as if she was propelling the sound from far within. The same deep place where her contempt for almost everyone seemed to come from. Babcia's teeth stayed clenched. Her lips barely moved. She spoke like a ventriloquist doll.

Margot seemed somewhere else, absent-minded. She slowly drew some flowers that she carried up to her nose. She was ignoring Babcia entirely. Margot had such incorrigible spirit. How Margot didn't feel or at least react to the aftershock of Babcia, I didn't know.

'It's okay, Babcia,' Margot replied, brushing Babcia's remark sideways as if it were an annoying fly. 'Besides, I'm sure I haven't missed anything.'

Babcia waved a violent, dismissive hand motion toward Margot.

Margot grinned calmly, looked around at us all and said, 'It's so humid; you feel like you're growing if you're standing still.'

'A summer's night … at least we've skipped the rain. That wouldn't have gone very well,' said Remy.

Margot smiled back at him, saying hello with her eyes. 'True.'

I'd watched Babcia with Margot many times. Two strong women; perhaps one wanting to do harm, the other not. In my opinion, Babcia oscillated between liking and very much disliking Margot. Babcia could not presume her throne with Margot, and I dared say that somewhere, deep down, Babcia respected that.

'I love her growl and bark,' Margot had once said to me during one of our precious times together here at the Narcissus Gardening Club. 'I relish it … her antics … her bite.' I hadn't followed her. Where I felt startled by Babcia, Margot evidently felt fascinated. 'Come on …' she'd said. 'Babcia's wonderful; she's ridiculous; have you ever met such a character?'

I had to agree on this point, although I'm not sure my nerves wanted to spend too much time with someone who had such towering presence as Babcia.

'This must be Niles.' Margot said.

Niles placed his hand on hers as they shook hands, 'I've heard so much about you. Anna is a bit of a fan.'

'Niles!' I couldn't help myself.

'What?' he said. 'It's great that you've found some

quality friends here.' Margot just smiled with civility toward him. She was strangely silent.

Remy stepped in and with a quizzical look said, 'Margot, this is William, he's new … he just came along tonight.'

Now we were all studying this tall, lanky fellow who stood a little away. His engaging eyes flicked a smile to Margot.

'Oh Remy, we have a very small world here,' said Margot. 'William is my dearest friend.' With this, she approached William and gave him a warm embrace. He hugged her back with a little less gusto. 'And here we find ourselves together at the Narcissus Gardening Club.' Her grin somehow got even larger. 'Tonight, will be more interesting than I'd anticipated.' Her hands moved to cup his jawline. 'Far more interesting.'

CHAPTER II

Margot casually presented her flowers to the group; they were roses, a gift from her neighbour.

'Do they smell?' Babcia asked. 'Roses must smell!'

'I'm afraid not, Babcia, but they're a striking red, aren't they.'

Babcia scoffed, 'A flower without a smell is like a man without a soul.'

'Oh well, we'll just have to enjoy their soulless beauty then, won't we,' said Margot not skipping a beat. 'Right, well … I'm sure we all have plenty to do. I'll join you as soon as I've gone down to The Hub and found a vase of some description.'

'There are glass bottles in there,' instructed Babcia, pointing to the quaint garden shed that adjoined the Birch Circle.

'Thank you, Babcia,' said Margot with a genuine smile. 'I'll just be a moment.' On her way she motioned to me to follow her. It was only a discreet glance, but that's all the encouragement I needed.

We were only steps away, when Margot leaned into

me and whispered, 'Why did you bring him here … Niles?'

I replied with a sad nod. 'Yeah I know, I'm really pissed off. I mean … this is my island.'

'So, what's going on?'

'I didn't want to bring him. He just came.'

We entered the small timber hut, where there was just enough light to look around for our excuse of a vase. 'Come on Anna, you could've stopped him, surely.'

I loved and hated that Margot cut through the crap you told yourself. I often felt naked with her. I felt supported and disarmed at the same time.

'You know, I really don't have a clue,' I said after a moment's thought. 'It's true, I did ultimately let him follow me here. I just couldn't be bothered with the fight.'

'That's fair enough.'

'Perhaps it's some sort of last scene before the curtain comes down.'

There was a faint grimace in Margot's expression.

I continued, 'Yeah, I can't explain it to be honest. Maybe I'm bringing him into my world to show him that I'm my own person … that I have my own life, even if it's this odd tribe. I wish I made more sense.'

'Well stand in line, beautiful!' Margot said lightly. 'There's not much sense to be had around here.'

I then back-pedalled. 'It's not such a big deal that he's here. I shouldn't carry on like he's an abuser or anything – not physically. He's only been a bit handsy—'

'Anna!' Margot said, then softened her tone. 'He throws things at you!'

'Yes, toward me … they don't make contact … only a few times.'

'A few?'

'Well …'

'And he stands over you?'

'Yes.'

'And he blocks your way and corners you?'

'Well a bit … sometimes … but he's never hit me. It sounds strange, but if he did … it'd make it easier to leave … It'd be … you know … more clear.'

Margot was shaking her head, a pained look on her face. 'Anna … this is all not okay. Anytime someone uses their body or uses objects to intimidate you, to have power over you … it's physical violence. Anna, psychological abuse is arguably even worse.' My eyes locked with hers. 'Anna … I've told you this before.'

We ended with an embrace, a knowing embrace between us. It's true, she had said these words before, but I hadn't been ready to hear them. But something had changed. Now I was finally ready. I'd touched base with Margot, and it felt good. Kind of like fuelling up.

As we casually wandered back to the group, I noticed Margot briefly lean toward William as he stood there awkwardly. With a mischievous smile, I heard Margot in a delicate, wafting voice say, 'You're in your "look casual" uniform?'

Margot and William briefly nodded to each other and then went their separate ways. My curiosity grew. Margot fascinated me more and more as I got to know her.

Tabitha then approached to corner Margot on our return. She looked at Margot with her nose raised to the air and her lips held with pursed determination. 'I thought you would put in a little effort, Margot. We're finally here without any danger of dirt or digging and you … you're still wearing sneakers. I thought you would be wearing something a little more appropriate for a party.'

'Do you mean heels?' said Margot, laughing. 'Sorry you'll never catch me wearing those. Shoes are for walking in, my friend. Quite simple.'

'Pha!' exclaimed Tabitha. 'You're no lady!'

'And I'm very partial to finding every opportunity for a lovely stroll,' Margot continued without encouragement. 'A walk in the night garden perhaps?'

'So unbecoming, those shoes!'

'Really?' said Margot, 'I think these are cute.' She tapped her black canvas shoes together playfully.

In her most indignant tone, Tabitha scoffed, 'There's no point talking with you, Margot.'

'Yes, Tabitha, it's just terrible … shocking. I'm nothing but a disappointment for you.'

If Tabitha was ready to leave the topic, Margot was clearly not. Tabitha was a lightweight compared to

Margot. In her twenty odd years as a clinical psychologist, no doubt Margot had learned how to deal with all types, from prima donnas to the seriously vexed and everyone in between. 'It's amazing how often you can fit in a walk or a wander,' Margot said. 'I find that the more peculiar the wander and the more lost I feel, the better.'

Tabitha gave a final flick of her head toward the stars and walked off. Margot again found a reason to smile.

*

The hairs on my neck bristled as I felt Niles approach from behind. He whispered in my ear. 'By process of elimination, you call Margot "The Goddess".'

I let out a deep exhale. *Here we go.*

'I thought the Goddess would be some real beauty.' He was still banging on about my pet-names for the Garden Club members. This was a thread that he could pull on.

But this time I actually wanted to respond. 'She is beautiful, Niles … inside and out. When you get a sense of her as a person, she has amazing energy … I adore her.'

This parked him and his face turned to stone. He glared at me. I enjoyed this although it left my heart pounding a little. He was finding out that I had beautiful people around me and deep affection for them. He'd hate this; it meant that I had strength from others. I wasn't as alone and vulnerable as he thought.

Margot had a classic elegance to her with her thick, wavy, dark hair halfway down her back and a delicate face. She had subtle, smiling wrinkles around her intense blue eyes. I loved that she was matter of fact about this. She wasn't precious. Margot said, 'They're a memento of all my good times.' As a woman, I truly envied the confidence that Margot brought to her curves. She'd worked out what suited her body and she wore it well. Margot went where her mood took her and paid little attention to how others viewed her. I always noticed what she was wearing. That day, she'd arrived wearing casual, black capri jeans, a sleeveless black turtleneck top and a striking baby blue and deep red oversized silk scarf. And of course, practical – if shabby – shoes. Whenever I spiralled into self-doubt about how I looked, I'd think of Margot, and her attitude grounded me. Ever since I'd met Margot, I'd adopted her into my internal world. The world made sense and looked beautiful through my Margot eyes.

The party whirred into action. Like a ring master, Babcia had orchestrated everyone's tasks.

'Dean!' she commanded. 'Collect the brooms. Remy and William, we need chairs. Fetch the chairs from The Hub!'

'Fetch! Hah!' Niles sneered.

Babcia was on a roll. 'Jacob …'

But Jacob had already scuttled off. He wouldn't be commanded by Babcia this time. He was following

Remy and William to The Hub. I watched, amused by his odd little skipping motions as he tried to keep up with William's and Remy's long strides. He was a living garden gnome.

As the others squabbled about who would do what errand, I also chose to exit and follow the men at a distance. Jacob eventually fell into step just behind Remy. Like an annoying pest, he made his inevitable launch. 'So, Remy, what's your deal? Are you gay?' Jacob clearly thought he was being smart.

Remy replied swiftly, without emotion. 'Jacob surely you've learned by your age that whether someone is straight or gay, it's none of your business. They're not accountable to you to tell you.'

Jacob fell silent. Remy turned to him with a perplexed look, a frown. 'A better question might be, are you kind? Are you an asset to people around you? Are you mindful of others? Now that's a useful question, Jacob, a relevant question.'

'I don't know what you're talking about.' Jacob turned away from Remy like a petulant child.

'Well, there you go!' Remy grinned looking down to him.

I marvelled at Remy's composure. Remy was holding up a mirror to Jacob, and Jacob didn't know which way to look. Jacob turned briskly and almost knocked me over as he waddled past back to the group. I was invisible to him, and the idiot had no idea that he'd thrown me off balance into the wall of camellias.

William reached me before Remy could, and he extended a helping hand. 'Are you okay?'

'Yeah, fine. I'm fine.' I waved him off as I gathered as much composure as I could muster. While I was intrigued to have a moment with Margot's strange friend, I hadn't planned on it starting off with me extracting myself out of shrubbery. I laughed it off in an effort to convince myself as much as him that I wasn't actually the bundle of nerves I felt like. I was just so wired and charged with tension.

William gave me my space and wandered back to Remy. 'That was well done Remy … with Jacob,' William said as we entered The Hub. 'To think on your feet like that, and cut him off. You went straight to the core.'

'I had a brute of a cousin growing up. Big on the put-downs but short on the brains. I'm afraid that I've had a lot of practice.'

William extended Remy a friendly smile. Together we decided on the chairs that were in the best condition, that had less rain and leaf stain on them. We were taking our time. There was no rush to return to the group.

'And the darkness falls,' Remy said out of nowhere.

William asked the inevitable question. 'So … I imagine that there is a story behind the name, the Narcissus Gardening Club … quite a striking name.'

'Let's say a memorable name?' I said.

Remy was quick to jump on this. This was a favourite and stirring topic for the gardening members. 'It's a pretty meaningful name for Babcia.' He said. 'She doesn't see any humour for, shall I say, the peculiarity of it. I don't think she's ever heard of the term *narcissist* as we would think of it. You see, the narcissus is her family flower. It's on her coat of arms.'

'Really!' William looked surprised. 'There you go. I wouldn't have guessed that.'

There was a somewhat awkward silence. 'But how did she name the garden club? This community garden has been here longer than her, surely.'

'See this lighting we're walking by.' Said Remy. 'These chairs we're gathering, the tables we're about to sit at, our generous new compost system, our BBQ, actually the whole general upkeep of the community garden? It's not common knowledge, but that's all Babcia. When you make a substantial and ongoing charitable input, you get to give it a name, I guess. It was previously just called the Seville Community Garden, after the suburb.'

To my eye Remy appeared to be in his mid-thirties, but he was one of those people whose age was hard to guess. Watching him work in the garden, I'd noticed his broad shoulders were shaped by hard work, rather than gym repetitions. His body looked functional, not preened. I liked how he somehow looked handsome in a careless kind of way.

I'd always thought that when someone's relationship was in tatters that they might then look around – that *I'd* look around. That I'd be tempted to find love and affection somewhere else. But strangely, even though I was so drawn to Remy, I didn't truly let myself go there in my head. My life was such a mess; I was probably not wanting to complicate it even further. But no question … he'd be my pick. When I was near him, my head, my body and my heart was consumed by him. I felt like a schoolgirl, giddy. Nevertheless, it seemed that I must finish one chapter before I start another. I had to finish things. I had to finish this.

*

On our return, I grabbed a broom and decided to help Dean. I'd managed to shake Niles. Any conversation looked good to me in comparison. 'So, Dean, you're single, partnered, married?' I'd never cared to ask him or ponder this before.

From out of nowhere Dean spat back, 'Well, I'd be married if she wasn't a lying, cheating bitch!'

I felt like I was going to vomit. Tears came immediately to my eyes. I'd been delicately balancing my whirling headspace, and this just tipped me over. I gaped at Dean. The group behind me instantly hushed.

He glared at my paled face. 'I won't be censored, especially bullshit, feminist censorship.' He needed no invitation to continue. 'She's got what she wanted; she's got the kids,' he growled. 'I only see them on the week-ends, and now she thinks she has a right to my money! My money? Well, she's in for a shock.'

I woke up from my frozen state. How many conversations tonight would I need to escape? 'Hey, I didn't mean to open up a can of worms, Dean. Sorry, happy to leave it,' I said. My tears were settling. The group were to my back. My delicate state was still my secret.

But he kept talking, barking more like, 'I won't be silenced about this … pretentious ego political correctness. I've got nothing to hide. She just up and left. *No reason.* There was nothing wrong. It was completely out of the blue. My wife just doesn't respect commitment. When I said till death do us part, I meant it. She's just weak. Weak! But you know what? Because she's weak, I know someone got into her head, someone told her to leave, and that person will pay!'

Then I snapped. A snap from deep within me. Instant heat flushed to my face. 'People don't just leave without a reason Dean.' My voice was shrill and gasping. 'You're kidding yourself if that's what you think! It's hard to leave. Really hard. They leave for a good reason. They leave because the situation is *crap*!' I yelled. Tears of anger flowed. 'They leave because it's been crap for too long, and they don't want their future to be crap, and they don't deserve for their life to be crap!'

Dean glared at me.

I couldn't stop. 'No one deserves to have their heart

and their head stomped on, abused day in and day out! Till death do us part!' I scoffed. 'You were probably her death! You were probably killing her on the inside day by day. Eroding her soul. Is this the kind of death that you're talking about? Is it Dean?'

I felt the group staring into my back. Silence.

Then the weirdest thing happened. Dean resumed what he was doing as if nothing had happened. He picked up the broom and kept sweeping. This jolted me, and I'm sure the group. Had this really just happened? His transformation completely undermined the punch in the gut that I had experienced and my subsequent outburst.

Then as absolute proof he was ignoring me, he started speaking coolly. 'Yes … my wife's just weak. She started to say, "Don't call a wolf out of the woods." The stupid woman keeps saying this, over and over again. I was too much of a force for her. I am a wolf and if she can't handle me, that's her problem. But now she'll pay and anyone who helps her … will pay too.' He was nodding away at himself, agreeing with himself, cheering himself on.

He was so altered, from volatile anger to calm. Even his sweeping seemed calm and methodical. A chill ran through me, up my spine. What had just happened?

I heard a chortle-type laugh from Jacob. 'Wow, relax everyone. We're here to relax, aren't we? This is a gardening club for goodness's sake. Be relaxed!'

William calmly walked in and stood between Dean

and I. 'Where do you think we should put these chairs, Dean?' Dean took a moment and then motioned toward some cleared areas.

I turned and walked. I needed to breathe, to get some air. Out of the corner of my eye I saw that Jacob was standing there looking very pleased with himself. I'm sure he thought that he'd just de-escalated the situation.

I found myself, with Niles as my shadow, automatically walking toward Remy. I needed comfort. If Niles didn't have Remy marked as a threat, he did now. I didn't care. Tonight at home, Niles would tell me how Remy was such a loser for just having a gardening job. He'd snarl and say that Remy was only pretending to get along with me. Why would he want to be my friend? It was only because his alternative company was the hideous old lady. Yep, tonight he would paint Remy as having lecherous intentions. He'd try to destabilise me, to create doubt in my mind. A good day for him was a day when Anna felt insecure, I was sure of it.

Lowering his head to meet my eyes, Remy whispered, 'Are you okay?'

With a grimace, I replied, 'Actually, I'm not … I'm not okay, but I will be.'

'Yes, you will.'

*

Momentarily calmed, I continued with my token sweeping. My broom was my ally. I held on tight, happy to have something to occupy me. I eyed Dean over at the other side of the Birch Circle. Surely anyone with any wit could tell that he was a controlling idiot. I felt sorry for his children.

My peace was short lived. Niles launched at me, 'Why do you come here, Anna?'

His head jerked at me like a chicken. He curled his nose in disgust. I was surprised that he wasn't saving his reproach for when we got home. 'They're all pathetic!'

While I'd been ambushed by Dean, I was ready for *this*. Niles' opinion felt like annoying white noise. 'They're my gardening family,' I said lightly, taunting him.

'Family? All families are a pain in the arse Anna! But you wouldn't know anything about that, because you don't have any family.' Niles was off and running. 'I'm sure if you did have any family, they would be a pain in the arse too. It's what families do! You're an only child, your father was an only child, and your mother was an only child, so you just don't know.'

My voice was low and firm. 'Niles, I know you're not actually going to listen to what I'm about to say, but I'll say it anyway. Firstly, you're incredibly insensitive … I was blessed to have my mum for most of my life. And yes, I never knew my dad, but I had my beautiful mum, and my mum's mum. But most importantly, I have our two children. So, I do know family.'

'What about me?'

I didn't acknowledge these last few words. 'Niles really,' I said with a sigh, 'you just don't like people, and you don't like being around people. Perhaps you and Babcia have more in common than you realise!'

Niles looked momentarily startled; this comparison clearly irritated him. 'What, the Queen and I?'

I stood looking directly at him. 'You don't have friends, Niles. You don't even like me to have friends or the kids to have friends over. So how can family have any chance? I'm not saying your family are my favourite people, but they're okay. You just write them off because they fit within the "people" category, and you don't like people!'

'How would you know what it's like to have family?' he said. He apparently hadn't heard a word I'd said. 'I'm sorry you're an orphan, Anna, but face it, how would you know what it's like to have a family?'

'I'm not an orphan! That's ridiculous … you're not an orphan when you lose your mum as an adult!' I shook my head; could I be bothered with this conversation? 'I know what the love of a family is, because I know what love is Niles.'

Niles again said, 'What about me? I'm your family.'

I shot back, 'In my book, family are people who love you and build you up, not tear you down.'

Niles suddenly changed gear. 'You talk about love,' he said. 'You don't show me love. When is the last time we had sex? You won't even have sex with me!'

'Why would I want to have sex with you?' I said in a heated whisper. 'You're not even nice to me!'

'Why would I be nice to you, when you don't have sex with me?' Niles' face looked as childish as his comment.

'Niles, people are nice to each other because they're nice people, not because they get something out of it. You don't be nice to someone to have sex with them. You're kind to someone because you're a kind person, full stop!'

Our conversation fortunately came to a sudden stop as people approached. I walked away promising myself yet again that I wouldn't get drawn into another pointless conversation with him. I had resolved not to talk to him tonight, hadn't I? Why did I allow myself to get drawn in again? Somehow, I was left more furious with myself than with him.

I could feel Niles continuing to glare at me. I doubt that he was reflecting on any of my words. I was sure he was just focussed on the fact that he was losing his grasp on me. Here I was talking back. I wouldn't at home mind you, but here were there were eyes on him, I was safe.

*

I took my opportunity and walked at pace from Niles' glare through one of the paths that tunnelled out of the Birch Circle. I was trying to breath in enough air. I felt a gasping urge to find some calm as my head spun. I hated how Niles had this effect on me. I felt like I was drowning and he was pulling me down. Drowning as anxiety took hold of my body, and my head fought to have any clear thoughts, to have any hope that my future would get better, that our kids' future would be better.

My feet took me to a bench in the fruit orchard. I sat, collapsing more like. It was a dark corner with just a dapple of moonlight. The smells of fresh and rotting citrus met me in equal measure. I was hidden behind a tree that I could've named in an instant in the daylight and with a clear head. Now it stood as a protective barrier between me and the world. I'd sat there many times; it was perhaps my favourite spot. I racked my brain, trying to visualise the detail by day, glad of a project for my mind, a distraction. There were steps approaching, coming from the arbour opening. Pulsating tension rose again in my chest. Strangely, I was happy to take this as another distraction; I'd be further from Niles in my head. Who was it?

An enormous sigh rolled out of me as I heard Margot's soft laugh. Although I couldn't see her, I knew she'd have her sweet smile; you couldn't laugh like that without smiling. I mirrored her smile and I felt my body begin to release. My comfort blanket had arrived.

'Obviously you're here for work?' I heard Margot say.

'Yes.'

I jolted, realising that she had a companion with her, William. I could see their two silhouettes.

'Well, I'm not here for work, William. So please don't put me to work too!' she said.

'I'll try not to.' I could hear a grin in his voice. 'Remy explained the rather intriguing name to me, the Narcissus Gardening Club. I don't know what to make of all this, Margot. She's a character, isn't she. You all call her Babcia?'

'Absolutely,' Margot replied with warmth. 'I find her … it's hard to put words around … luminous. I find her character to be luminous. Babcia *truly* intrigues me.'

I could hear a gentleness in his voice. 'Yeah, I can see that she'd hold your interest, for sure. You like the peculiar, Margot, something to chew on. But … luminous, really?'

'Absolutely!'

Then he said it. I heard the words, 'I'm not too sure about Niles being here though … Anna's husband. Bit of a worry there.'

'Why?' Margot said instantly.

'Well—'

'No, no, I'm not in work mode. We agreed!'

'Sure, no problem.'

'But I can't not be curious now.'

'Yeah but Margot … seriously … when are you not in work mode?' They both shared a playful laugh. I wasn't laughing. My stomach was in my throat. My high alert with Niles had just received some version of proof. My head spun.

'Just leave it with me,' Margot said. 'Let me see if I can join the dots.'

'Sure … sure.'

There was silence between them. Margot cleared her throat. 'But William, to know Babcia you have to know her history—'

'Go on,' he said.

Margot might have changed direction in their conversation, but my mind stayed laser focussed on William's comment. Why was it bad news that Niles was here? How did this stranger know of Niles?

Margot spoke again. It was clear that this wouldn't be brief. She began with the sort of tone that you use at the beginning of a story. 'Babcia has experienced a lot of loss, the death of her only child, and her husband … but to truly know Babcia you have to go back to her childhood … growing up during very harsh times in Poland.'

'Do tell.' William had a solemn tone about him.

I was wondering about my situation. Here I was eavesdropping. This was becoming extremely awkward. I wish I'd jumped in straight away. But now I felt almost stupefied, so wracked with indecision. I huddled there quietly hoping they'd just walk on. My initial curiosity to listen rapidly became overtaken by guilt.

'Both her parents died. She had one sister, but she was separated from her sister when she was very young. Her sister was sent to live with an aunt.'

'Pretty sad beginning.'

Margot pushed on, 'Yes … now what's important to know is that she's eighty-two.'

'Yes, I know, born 1939,' William replied. This information was somehow fresh for him.

'I could ask you how you know that, but I won't,' Margot said. As I listened to their conversation, I was again consumed by curiosity. They were so in synch; both their conversation and how they seemed to appear so comfortable in each other's presence and, I don't know, kind of flowing. I felt a shot of jealousy. It would be quite something to be that close to Margot.

'Well … Babcia was born just when World War II was about to savage Poland. She was then orphaned just as Poland was set to try to recover from the ashes of the war. They were incredibly harsh and deprived times. We can't truly understand. Us Australians, we're so sheltered here.'

'True.'

'I don't know what happened to her parents … I'm sure that's a whole other story.'

'Something horrible I'd imagine. I mean, they were probably our age when they died.'

'No, a lot younger …'

There was silence as they walked further away. I was so glad that they hadn't walked closer toward me. I was committed now to staying silent.

At a stretch I could still hear them.

'This tree's my favourite,' Margot said. 'They were clever to put this avocado tree so far away. It's huge; we should lop the top off it so that we can pick all the avocados, not just the bottom fruit.'

'Wouldn't that look weird?' asked William. 'It would look like a flat top.'

'It'd be fun to find out.'

I could barely hear them now. So much for not wanting to listen. I was hooked. Reaching to not miss a word, I heard William then say, 'Yeah, well, Bridie says that the only tree she wishes we had is an avocado tree.'

'Absolutely.'

'So, you were saying that Babcia got separated from her sister,' William said.

'Yes, when she was a very young child, she was sent to live with an uncle. But this was a raw deal for her. From her stories, it sounds like she was utterly neglected. She was the Cinderella with her cousins, except with no happy ending.'

'Pretty tough.'

'From what I can make of it, she grew up being resented. Another mouth to feed. Hard times. Explains why she can be like barbed wire.'

'She told you all this?'

'Yeah. Bit by bit over time. Sometimes while talking, sometimes while she was throwing some offensive comment at me,' Margot said with a gentle chuckle.

'Understandable.'

'She told me that … when she was young, this is post-war Poland now, that when she was told to run an errand, or sent out to work, they wouldn't leave the door open for her for when she got back. There would be a ladder.'

'A ladder?'

'Yeah, she'd have to climb a ladder and pry open a high window to get back inside. Imagine, Poland's bitter winter. She said her hands would burn from the cold. Imagine how dangerous that would be … a child climbing a slippery ladder with numb fingers. She was literally shut out from her family.'

There was silence. I hoped they wouldn't walk further away; I wanted to hear more. I wanted to hear how Babcia went from being an impoverished orphan to being here, on the other side of the world.

Fortunately, they had only wandered a bit to the side; they were actually getting closer to me now. 'It sounds like her street survival skills came into play as an adult,' Margot continued. 'When she married her husband, she steered her life to become a mercenary businesswoman, and she drove the new market of domestic storage. A new commodity for the new world.'

'And came to Australia?'

'Yeah … and came to Australia,' Margot said. 'But, William, you said *you* had something to tell *me*. Something about Babcia's family—'

Footsteps were approaching from the arbour

walkway, and Margot and William fell silent.

'Hello?' the voice called.

It was Remy. I felt so relieved. Here was my opportunity. Hoping that he'd momentarily distracted them, I walked from the darkness, looking like I had arrived from one of the many Birch Circle passages that led into the gardens. This was my plan anyway.

My frazzled energy was soothed by Remy's outstretched arms. He gave me a friendly hug. 'How are you?'

'Yeah … I'm fine.' I said the lie that we say so often.

I looked from his, to Margot's face framed from the moonlight. She had a sad smile. I didn't want her to be real with me right then. I felt the tension in my chest return; it had become like a roommate to me lately. I carried around this wound-up energy, and all I needed was the slightest tip-off and the elephant would return to my chest. Feeling my heartbeat had become strangely normal to me.

'Hello Anna, Remy,' William said. 'We were just enjoying the orchard. I'd better get back.' He didn't stop in his stride and with a polite nod, to Remy and I, he strolled at pace past us.

'I'm sorry, Margot. I didn't mean to intrude,' Remy said.

'No, not at all. The circus is gathering,' she said with a laugh.

We stood together in comfortable silence for a

moment, looking at the trees stirring in unison in the wind. It was so peaceful, they were dancing a slow movement. It wasn't windy, just a gentle breeze. Just enough to inspire a wind chime. The trees sang their song.

It seemed that we were in no hurry to go anywhere. This quietness, a moment to treasure.

'You know,' said Remy softly, 'I was thinking … even with all of our chats here at the garden, I don't actually know what you do for work, Margot.'

'Our chats … hah! You mean Remy … while you stand there helplessly while Babcia criticises my gardening skills?' Margot joked.

'Well … yeah.' Remy bowed his head sheepishly, his eyes slowly returning to Margot.

'I'm a psychologist, a clinical psychologist,' said Margot simply. She caressed the leaves of a citrus tree. She reached for some infant flowers, crushing them and smelling them. Before Remy could respond, Margot continued with a mocking tone, 'I've heard it a million times … the usual responses are: "I don't know how you do that, Margot. I couldn't listen to people's problems all day." Or "Are you analysing me?" Or "I'd always thought about being a psychologist because people tell me their troubles".'

Remy was smiling, nodding.

'Don't get me wrong,' Margot said reassuringly, 'I absolutely love my job, my profession, but it's a far cry from what people think psychology is. I mean it's extremely meaningful, and it's only dull if it's not challenging, and it's usually challenging.'

'I'd believe that,' Remy said.

'But you know,' continued Margot, 'I don't tell people that I'm a psychologist as a rule.'

'Why not?' I said.

'Because too many people either start telling me the story of when they saw a psychologist, how they need to see a psychologist, or as I said, how they've always wanted to be a psychologist. Worse still, they value me because they see me as a professional and I absolutely hate that.'

Remy was grinning and nodding. 'So, if someone asks what you do, what do you say?'

'I say I work in retail,' chirped Margot with ease, a quick rise of her shoulders.

'No!' said an incredulous Remy.

'Absolutely, and then we can move on. Works a charm.'

Somehow, we were walking back again to the arbour. 'Better go before Babcia cracks her whip,' Margot jeered.

'Absolutely,' said Remy, 'But you know, when we can steal another moment, I have another question, if you don't mind.'

*

No sooner had we re-entered the Birch Circle than Niles was again by my side. He smiled and put an arm around me; I felt a chill. *Don't do that again.* Was what he was saying with the pressure of his fingers on my shoulder. *Don't go off; stay here with me.*

Tabitha approached in rapid succession. She motioned toward Dean. 'He's a bit much, isn't he?'

'Sorry?' I said wincing. The most 'too much' person I had ever met was pointing her finger at another.

Tabitha didn't need encouragement. 'Dean knows nothing about relationships. He's a brute.' We were having an in-depth conversation out of nowhere. She just started as if she was already mid-sentence. 'But I know love. Love is tragic.' Tabitha wasn't speaking to Niles or I now, she'd turned, raised her voice and was speaking to the whole group. Her exaggerated manner ensured that she had everyone's attention. What had I walked into?

'I've known tragic love,' she said with great theatrics. I felt immediately embarrassed for her. She was being ridiculous. 'Love that wasn't meant to be. It breaks your heart; it breaks you. And then you live in pieces.' I saw Remy shift uncomfortably, even Jacob look at his shoes.

'You have not lived until you have loved as deeply as I have,' Tabitha continued not discouraged. 'There are those who don't know love; they just take people hostage.'

'Go Princess, go,' said Niles, laughing in my ear. 'Is she serious? She's a crackpot. This is fantastic!'

I think the Garden Club members on the whole had

become practiced at avoiding Tabitha's antics. We all knew her erratic rants. I watched as Dean, Remy and Margot turned from her. Poor, uninitiated William just stood there looking confused, thinking he was obliged to be polite. Babcia sat on her throne, glaring. Eventually Tabitha came to the end of her performance. There was no applause, just mystified exhaustion.

*

There was still a general buzz of activity, a whole lot of fussing, people going in circles, looking busy, all with Babcia barking ineffective orders.

Margot raised an eyebrow at me. I jumped at the unspoken invitation to again join her as she stepped away from the group.

'Anna!' Niles commanded as Margot and I exited the party together.

'Come get the lights from my car?' Margot asked.

'Absolutely,' I said. My feet were almost skipping toward her.

As we strolled, I inhaled the familiar scent of jasmine. 'Please help me understand,' I said. 'That was weird even for her. What the hell was that with Tabitha and her tragic love tale?'

'Impressive little foray,' said Margot. 'But I dare say that she wasn't talking about her husband, sorry her ex-husband.'

'Go on,' I urged.

'Well, we all know … heard too many times in fact, that Tabitha was married and then separated. We also know that she had a lover who she was besotted with.'

'Okay?' This was news to me. Trust Margot to get the backstory on everyone. She wasn't a gossip … exactly. She was more like a beagle who just couldn't help but be interested in what was happening around her.

Margot was picking the jasmine flowers and smelling their delicate scent. 'What is interesting is the time-frame, from what I can make out. She was married, an affair started, the affair ended not by her, her marriage ended not by her. It sounds like things didn't go as Tabitha planned. It sounds like a Tabitha mess. And she calls it a love story … it sounds like a shipwreck. I can't count how many times she has bleated a nostalgic, melodramatic version of this to me. And I'm here for some lovely down time, to just enjoy the quiet gardens. I'm surprised you've missed her line of fire with this one. It's all very sad, in every direction.'

'Sad and annoying!'

'Yes, absolutely.'

We walked on. We were in no rush. 'I hear that you and Niles have brought the barbecue supplies; that's very kind of you,' said Margot.

'No, that's not the case at all.' I was quick to correct her. 'I just bought the drinks … the punch ingredients. Babcia bought all the food … the meat, bread rolls and salads; all ordered and paid for. She even had half the bread rolls pre-buttered before I picked them up. She thought of everything … the serving utensils, the sauces, everything. I just picked them up for her. She's very generous, but she doesn't want anyone to know that she's putting this on … food wise. It's all very strange, and now I'm going to get all the credit!'

'Well, you're doing Babcia a great service then. She can't afford to wreck her image, can she?'

I conceded this and then gazed off at the swaying shadow of trees that looked ethereal in the moonlight. In the simple act of stopping to absorb all that was around me, I was being rewarded with an abundance of sights, smells and even feels. Feeling the breeze, feeling the crispness, even velvet softness of the greenery around me. Authors who write of enchanted gardens shouldn't get the literary credit; the poetry is already with the plants.

Margot turned squarely to me; her eyes pierced mine. Somehow, she conveyed deep compassion and knowingness with this simple glance. 'Now, my beautiful, how are you?'

I was not planning to *go there* with Margot that night. But you couldn't be false with Margot; you just couldn't. She saw through my best efforts in a moment. Like a dam that suddenly broke loose, I started to speak at an absolute gallop. Different thoughts overlapped each other, often in a disjointed way. It was just pouring out of me. I spoke with urgency. I didn't know how long

I would have alone with her. My words came in a loud whisper, with stretches of angry tears.

'I'm done with Niles having his foot on the back of my neck.' With this, Margot beckoned me to the closest seat. We were on the outskirts, hopefully safe in privacy. 'All of the threads that made up our relationship have broken. Gone. All of them. Ages ago really … I just kept gluing it back together, by trying to keep the peace … you know.'

Margot looked straight into my eyes. I felt her hand delicately move some strands of hair from my face, gently willing me to share more. 'Now that I'm stepping back, I'm realising so many things, like my stress is completely linked to Niles' stress and he's always stressed. He's a control freak but more and more he's got no real control so he's not coping. He isn't coping with the fact that he's failing, for years now, failing at his business.'

'Right?'

'It's strange, he's always talking things up, but there's never any action. He doesn't cope, and he doesn't communicate … no consideration. Everything just goes around and around so that you never get anywhere, and you know what else I've recently realised?'

'What?'

'He just cuts me down to cope. Either just straight cutting me down or in a weird "humorous" way. That's what he thinks anyway. He tells me that I don't know how to take a joke. He thinks humour is cutting me down or cutting others down.'

'Critical humour,' Margot said, 'but it's *not* humour; it's just criticism.'

I wanted to get it all out. This was my overflow moment. It was the smashing of the old me with the new me, like when saltwater meets fresh. I was churning with movement within. I almost needed to talk in point form to cover it all. Margot just listened. She listened with kindness and care. 'He deflects; he's a master at that. He kicks the dog when he's stressed.'

'You're the dog?'

'I'm the dog. And he twists everything I say. Twists it around. And then after his storm, it's like everything is supposed to be okay. He behaves as if nothing has happened, as if he hasn't bruised me, pummelled me, emotionally you know. I've learned to just shut up; I have to sweep it under the mat. Ignore it.'

'Ignore what?' Margot asked.

'Me. My hurt.'

'Of course.' Margot nodded sadly.

'Then he just starts up again whenever he feels like it and goes in for another round.'

'You can't win,' Margot said.

'You've got it. I can't win. Those times that I've had it in me to say … *I've had enough, I'm out* … then.' My voice began to shriek. 'Then he's super considerate for perhaps half a day. That's it! Then he's cruel again! This shows that he knows what he's doing. He's capable … he can behave if he chooses to. He can fake being nice and that just makes it worse. He's letting himself be an arsehole … he's choosing this.'

I had more to go, tears were streaming down my face, and I didn't care. 'The way he speaks to me … I feel like nothing, invisible. I'm reduced to the size of a pea. He thinks everything is a personal attack on him. He accuses me of all sorts of paranoid bullshit.'

'He carries on like he's the captain,' Margot said, 'but he keeps crashing and blaming *you*. He gets angry at you for not shovelling the water out of the ship fast enough.'

'Exactly!' I said. 'And he's *never* wrong.'

'And the business?' Margot said carefully. 'Is it as bad as all that?'

I shrugged. 'He doesn't want my input. I've saved his bacon so many, many times – smoothing things over when he's offended staff. But he can never acknowledge it, and he won't let me see the finances. He's a dictator, simple as that.'

I tried to take a deep breath. My breath was matching the speed of my heart. I was starting to feel dizzy, but I had to continue. 'I'm at saturation point with all of this, Margot. I'm stepping through the exit. I've overridden him. I've been to the accountant. I can because my name is on everything. So he's really angry. But I don't care. But I do care … because I'm scared of him. But I have to untangle myself.'

I finally paused. Margot was holding both of my hands in hers.

'Take a moment, Anna, take a breath. You're starting to fade out on me.' Margot was stroking my cheek, wiping the tears as she went. Her touch was so soothing. I was glad we'd found our dark corner of the garden; it was just us, the dark sky, and the trees swaying gently. There were not many stars to see, but there were enough.

'Beautiful,' Margot gently said, 'none of this is okay and more to the point … it's not okay that he's okay with this.'

'I don't love him,' I declared flatly. We sat for a moment. It felt like a window of quiet after a storm. My voice was now almost hoarse. 'That love has been pummelled out of me.'

'Yes.'

'I worry for him though. He's going to be a mess without me propping him up.'

'Well, the first ingredient is for him to learn about himself, but I don't know if he would want to, that would mean owning his shit. You can nudge, but you can't make someone wake up to their stuff.'

I looked intently at Margot. 'You know I could even overlook his bad decisions and his going in circles if he treated me with a drop of respect and care.'

'Well, my lovely, you're precious, and you can't spend your years on this planet limping along and getting pummelled. You can't waste your life with someone who is not on your side. You should only have people in your world who deserve you, who really see you and who cherish you. You wouldn't want your daughter in this relationship, would you?'

'Hell no.'

'Well then,' replied Margot.

Our conversation fell into a natural lull. I felt numb, whirling thoughts were there, but I couldn't seem to access them. What I did feel was a distinct feeling of release. Margot gently put her arm around me, and I softened into her comforting hug. We sat for what felt like a long while, content in silence. I realised that I had calmed and with a knowing smile between us, we rose to fetch Margot's lights and walked in step back to the circus.

CHAPTER III

Upon our return, Margot and I were met with energy, tension and awkwardness from all directions. I could hear Babcia micromanaging small, tedious details; where someone had missed sweeping leaves … the exact positioning of chairs. Why we were sweeping up leaves in the first place was lost on me. Margot and I arrived with many tangled fairy lights, and the club members launched enthusiastically at a task to busy themselves. Many hands swarmed on the cobweb of cords.

From a distance, this would've looked like a parody of movement. There were perhaps five different sets of fairy lights, and their tangled state brought loud criticism from Tabitha.

'This is a mess.' Tabitha grabbed at them with force. 'This is a disgrace. Margot, how could you let this happen?' Her comments trickled on. At most she got a polite, awkward smile from William.

Babcia, however, jumped in and agreed with Tabitha's disapproval. Strangely, this annoyed and silenced Tabitha. There were hands and arms going in every direction with some members appearing to be dancing, weaving between each other. It looked a bit like a barn dance. From her chair, Babcia observed with only the occasional, unhelpful directive. At one point the group looked more tangled than untangled.

In amongst the chatter about how to untangle the lights, Jacob abruptly turned to Margot and I'm sure to the group's surprise, asked something meaningful, 'Narcissist? I've heard the word before. We all joke about the name of the garden club, but what is a narcissist?'

'Sorry?' asked Margot, understandably taken aback.

'I mean, sure, I've heard the word thrown around as an insult. I think it means you're full of ego.' This was a different approach for Jacob: actually asking a solemn question.

Margot was always a fan for putting information on the table. 'Well.' She took a deep breath to begin.

A pensive look washed over William's face. I was intrigued about where this was going to go. It was like this group of people were on a boat that was delicately balancing, with members who could tip it over at any moment. And here was Margot, classic Margot, about to address the elephant in the room. I wasn't at all sure that Babcia knew the meaning of this word shared with her family crest, not to mention her precious gardening club.

The usually playful Margot now stepped into her professional mode. 'Most people don't know what

Narcissistic Personality Disorder is Jacob. Do you know what it is?'

'Well … argh …'

Margot looked to the group. The startled faces suggested that many were not used to her carrying such a commanding voice. 'We don't say "a narcissist"; that's generally an insult or a throw away term. It's a diagnosis … a condition. We call it Narcissistic Personality Disorder, or Narcissistic PD or NPD for short, but never "a narcissist". Some people think they know what it is, but they really have no clue. To really know a person with NPD, you have to have experienced them, perhaps survived them … to understand.'

The silence in the leaf-lined room was deafening. 'You can't know what it feels like to be burned by fire until you have experienced it, can you? Or what it's like to be belted by a storm at sea, until you have survived it? It's the same with someone with Narcissistic PD. Unless you've had them in your life and survived them, you don't have the experience to draw on. You can't know their core, to truly get a sense of how they tick.'

Margot had everyone's attention. We continued untangling the lights, but silently and slowly, ears alert.

Margot continued, 'They're like the kid who thinks they own the whole sandpit; they take your toys, everything is for them, they don't share, and they don't give. But they're adults. It doesn't hurt them to hurt you. They think we must play by their rules; everything must be on their terms. They bully you, with mean words or by confusing you with their very, very clever twisting of your words or the situation. They think they're blameless or the victim. You're always to blame and somehow always a bad person. They are never wrong. There's a malignant sadness to them. They make it punishing to talk about issues. They rage at you or dismiss you if you try. So, you learn to stop trying. It's not only pointless, but dangerous to you. They want to erode you to the *size of a pea.*'

Margot had used *my* words. She glanced up at me at this moment, but then quickly moved on. I appreciated her gesture and her discretion.

All eyes were on Margot, her voice now kept up a low, quiet rhythm. 'They want to cut your confidence down, cut it out completely, then you'll be a suitable minion for them. You'll feel inferior, where you belong. Then they will have the power because you're so eroded. To a passing person they smile with the sweetness of charm … angelic. They only bully you when you're alone with them. They tell stories of their magnificent castles, but they just have sand. If you, by pure good fortune, happen to be having fun or doing something meaningful … pleasurable even … they will quickly put a stop to it! If something is important to you, then that is a threat to them … this becomes their new target. When they're kind to you or love bomb you … watch out. There's an agenda. You'll soon see. The kind front doesn't last long. A storm will follow.'

Margot seemed lost in her own thoughts as she continued to speak, 'This is all done with full awareness and full control.'

Boom. This hit me.

'The proof for this,' she continued, 'is that they know how they ought to behave. We know this because they can behave beautifully when under the eyes of the outside world. They're wolves in sheep's clothing. Most of the world see a sheep, but those who have learned this lesson, see through this woolly layer. The wool isn't pulled over their eyes! They see the clever wolf within.'

Margot had spoken with a strange matter of factness in her tone, leaving a heaviness in the mood within the Birch Circle. Margot had gone to a depth of conversation that I'm sure was unfamiliar to many present. I wondered how this would be received. There had been no comment, no reply from the group. Would Niles be wondering if she was talking about him? I'd often wondered about Tabitha, Jacob and Dean. Would they be looking at themselves in the mirror that Margot had just held up? My guess was that they didn't have any ... or not much awareness of their reflection. Were they just hearing a description that was relevant to others? There were no indignant comments; there was silence. Margot, true Margot, had cast her spell. She had the group in a trance, consumed by the story she had told, the story that unfortunately wasn't fiction.

*

Margot was evidently happy to leave the group to digest this information as they chose. I imagine that she wanted to get out of work mode and back to her lighter self.

She declared, 'Well, I better go get the extension cords for this lot from The Hub. Anyone want to help me?'

I walked toward her, but I saw her motion to William. My sigh was caught mid-flow when Margot flicked a quick raise of her eyebrows to me. I was going to sit at the big kids' table. I could tag along. What relief. Seamlessly, we slipped away. The remaining group was left to complete the last of the fairy-light sorting. Berating remarks returned between them.

The gentle crackle of our steps on the stones underfoot was interrupted by a sudden loud bark from Dean behind us, 'The proper way to do it is to loop it around … no, that's not how it's done.' A cranky, snapping reply from Tabitha and strangely Niles could be heard behind us as we walked away.

William looked at me awkwardly. I was imposing on them, but I really didn't want to be left back at the party.

'Anna is keen to join us, William … She's trying to avoid being alone with someone,' Margot said simply.

'Who?'

'My husband,' I said dryly.

William awkwardly grinned back.

'William, we can talk openly with Anna. I can vouch for her.'

'Margot … I trust you of course … your judgement … you know that, but I really don't know if …'

'Well, I plan to keep an eye on Anna for the night and help her sidestep Niles, so either we don't talk shop tonight or we talk with Anna. Your decision, but I assure you, it's fine.'

I felt horrible. I saw the look of strain on William's face, but I was determined not to go back to the party and have Niles be my shadow.

I tried to break the ice. 'That was an impressive explanation.'

'I didn't mean it to get personal,' Margot said. 'But if an opportunity arises to fight ignorance – well, I'll have a shot. I doubt it'll have any impact.' Margot turned to William. 'Well, you're not a gardener, William; I think Anna's worked that out.'

William grinned. We were at The Hub now, free from prying eyes. She gave him a quick hug, and a gentle nudge.

'No,' said William.

'And,' continued Margot, 'you don't even *like* gardens right?'

'Not especially. Bridie thinks that it's absolutely hilarious that I'm here, at a gardening club of all places,' said William.

Margot let out a bellow of laughter. 'Oh, Bridie!'

'Who's Bridie?' I asked.

'Bridie is William's wife, and my dearest friend, along

with William here.' She winked at him. 'It's wonderful to have your best friends married.'

And with that, the picture became clear. William was in Margot's inner, inner circle. My estimation of him shot up exponentially.

'So, you're here for work.' Margot returned to William. 'And somehow you managed to get membership here at the Narcissus Gardening Club.' Margot mocked an eye roll as she said the club name. 'That's hard to do, William. Pretty impressive footwork even for you.'

I agreed with an enthusiastic nod.

'I'm actually here with Babcia,' he said. 'As you might have put together. Babcia seems to be able to arrange all things, but I'm not … not a member, don't worry there. Once this is all over, I don't think you'll find me at a gardening club again.' He looked out to our surrounds. 'It is beautiful here though.'

'Once this is all over?' repeated Margot curiously.

William leaned his head toward her and spoke even more discreetly, 'We're always crossing paths … in work mode. I'm investigating a murder or some crime, and you're consulting regarding the players. Let's just hope that we don't have to work together again here. Let's hope it's all smoke and mirrors. It'd be nice to enjoy your company away from some crisis we're mopping up.'

What on earth were they talking about? Work mode?

Crisis? Crime? *Murder?* 'Sorry … what?' I said. 'What kind of crisis are you expecting?'

Margot and William glanced at each other. William shook his head. It was a tiny movement, and I probably wasn't supposed to see it, but I did.

'I'm sure it's nothing,' Margot said quickly. 'William's just being over-cautious as usual. Right … William?'

'Yep … yep, that's right,' he said.

William wasn't a very good liar whatever his work role here.

Margot nodded and said wryly, 'And I've come here to relax!' She laughed a slightly sad laugh which ended with a quiet sigh. 'You know William … I actually like some of the people here … some, not all.'

'Well … we'll see how tonight goes.'

'We'll help you out tonight, William, won't we, Anna? We'll be beyond discreet. We won't blow your cover by asking you any gardening questions.'

'Yeah, I'm hoping everyone is so busy with the party that they don't actually talk about gardening too much, otherwise I'll be completely lost'.

'I'll be your gardening wingman.' Margot wrinkled her nose playfully. 'I'll look after you. Perhaps I could teach you some impressive garden language to dazzle the members?'

William grimaced.

Something had caught her eye. 'Can you guess what this is?'

'You know I can't,' was his flat response.

'Well, let me tell you,' said Margot playfully, needing no encouragement. 'This is a Dibble Stick, yes, a Dibble Stick. A small hand tool for digging holes … for planting bulbs.'

'Right?'

'What's another fun one? Ha! A Pistil, I'm sure this will come in handy! Did you know a Pistil is the seed-bearing organ of a female flower!'

'Yeah, I'm sure I'll need to know that tonight, Margot. Thank you for your botanical lesson, but can we please stop now?'

I liked Margot and William's banter. Their ease could not have been more of a contrast to the whirring of thoughts that now consumed me. But who was William really?

'How are your boys?' William asked Margot, clearly changing the topic.

'They're great. Every day they become more man and less boy. Just more to hug. Takes some reaching, they're so tall, but they're the same teddy bears they've always been.'

He's here for work. 'Won't blow your cover?'

'Absolutely,' said William warmly. 'I can't believe how much they are growing up. And I mean up.'

Shaking her head with gentle thought, Margot said, 'They're a bit cranky at me at the moment, though.'

'Really?'

I mean, his comment, 'I'm not too sure about Niles being here. Bit of a worry there.' What was that?

'The dryer …' Margot leaned in my direction. 'Anna, do you think a dryer is essential?'

'What?' I spluttered.

'A dryer?' William asked.

'Yeah,' Margot didn't wait for my reply. 'I'm the only one who can get our dryer to work … It's on its last legs … pretty tricky. The boys can't get it to work. But …' She laughed. 'I don't want to replace the dryer because I want them to keep having to hang their clothes out. I think it's good for them … good training.'

'Margot!' William scoffed playfully.

'I mean I help them out if it's urgent … uniforms … all that … but they can't just rely on it. I think it's great.'

What could William's job be? Some sort of fraud investigator? I could believe that Niles wouldn't have a drop of conscience about doing something dodgy under the table … but I'd know surely, wouldn't I? And why would a fraud investigator come to a garden party?

'I think that's just great!' I said trying to look like I was part of their conversation.

'You do a great job, Margot, getting them to be young men, not big children,' William said.

'They probably think that I'm a tightarse with money … over the dryer,' she said.

What if Niles has done something criminal? Lost his

cool, got violent or something? He's got a violent temper for sure – but he usually leaves that for me, for at home. He's a coward out there in the world. Isn't he?

The banter went on, but I couldn't listen with more than half an ear. *What if Niles has some sort of double life? What if they're doing some deep investigation into him? But how would they know he would be here tonight? I didn't even know he would. I wouldn't have dreamed he would ever come here … Is William here for me? Impossible.*

William was absentmindedly playing with a small shovel he had found along the path. 'How's Cat and Kemper?'

This drew a hearty laugh from Margot. 'I'm impressed, William. Good on you! You remembered their names.' She gently punched his arm. 'They're ugly beautiful as ever. Thank you very much.'

The more questions I ask myself, the more the picture doesn't make any sense. My day-to-day life has had me balancing on knife edge with the tension at home, and now I have overheard William's ominous words of warning. My head was beginning to spin.

'Sorry, Anna.' Margot gestured to include me in the conversation. She needn't have bothered, as I was more interested in my own mental crisis. 'Cat and Kemper are my cats, my peculiar sphynx cats. William here doesn't like cats so he's humouring me beautifully.'

She turned again to William. 'How's our beautiful

Bridie? I haven't seen her for a couple of weeks, and how are the girls?' asked Margot.

'Good, good … Bridie and I are currently trying to teach them not to squeal. Trying at least. It really isn't necessary all this squealing … excruciating and incessant squealing. Can't stand. Is it just their age?' asked William.

Margot grimaced. 'You have a daughter, Anna, don't you?'

Margot had full knowledge that I had a young son and daughter. She was just including me in the conversation. With this, Margot was looking intently at me. Studying me. I momentarily tensed as she squeezed my shoulder. To brace myself even with Margot, my anxiety must have hit a new high. But it wasn't Margot I feared; it was Niles, my own husband. I had learned a long time ago that I wasn't safe with him, not emotionally, and sometimes not physically, but now the outside world …

'I'm not cut out to be the father of squealing girls. Happy to go to work if I'm honest.' William continued oblivious of Margot and my quiet exchange. 'They don't need to squeal. We'll get there. I just can't stand it.'

I cupped Margot's hand in mine as they talked. *I'm okay.* I gestured.

Margot changed direction with William again. 'Has Bridie convinced you to go camping yet? Last time we caught up she sounded pretty determined.'

'It's become even worse,' explained William with

a subtle frown at Margot's gestures of support and affection for me. I'm sure he didn't understand what was going on, but he was respecting my privacy. He continued with some desperation. 'Now she wants us to go camping by the beach!'

'That sounds wonderful!' exclaimed an enthusiastic Margot.

'Absolutely,' I managed to splutter.

'No, it's not! Two things I hate, camping and sand … fresh hell for me.'

So who was William? Who was this man? I strangely liked him, I couldn't help it, he seemed kind. He's Margot's close friend … But my gut clenched … I felt like William carried within him something that was going to make my world implode and I didn't need any help with that. Panic welled up in me. Was he a policeman? A private investigator? Someone with some government department? Who was this man and what relevance would he have for my world?

'Oh, you make me laugh,' Margot said. 'If this fresh hell ever happens, take a photo for me, otherwise I won't believe you.'

'Actually, it looks like she's going to have a win with the cats as well! We have our dogs, but no, no, no, they want cats, all three of them. The girls are blatantly ganging up on me. Why aren't Horatio and Houston enough?'

'Your dogs are lovely, but the heart wants what the

heart wants,' said Margot, now squeezing my hand. Maybe she presumed that I was a puddle of anxiety purely from the stress that I brought to the evening. Or did she know that her dear friend William was my final straw tonight.

They were going on about cats or camping or something. *He has to be a policeman,* I thought. *Surely. It's the most likely explanation and he's here on some sort of undercover police business relating to Niles. But since I was the only one guaranteed to be here tonight ... has Niles got me mixed up in this somehow? Has Niles done something and thrown me under the bus?* My free hand clenched the bench seat. The harsh edges of the timber pressed into my palm. This texture, this solid pressure against the softness of my hand was my rescue ... I squeezed it to the point of pain. I wanted to move from the pain in my head to the pain in my palm. I needed to calm down. I needed to escape.

It seemed that Margot and William could have continued with their banter forever, but they obviously felt obliged to keep our time away from the group limited. I slowly tried to follow them. Margot reached for me, a concerned smile. We made our way back to the group with more extension cords and adaptors than we could need.

She whispered to me, 'It's okay, darling. You don't have to go home tonight. Come and stay with me. Where are the kids?'

'They're at my friends' for the night. They're okay.'

'It's settled then.'

*

As Jacob and Niles returned to the group with ladders, Jacob began his interrogation. 'So, Niles, what do you do for a crust? What's your line of work?'

I'd seen Niles with his practiced response many times. He crosses his arms, moves his chin down, and leans back. On cue, this is exactly what he did. In his best, manly voice, with furrowed brow, he said with volume, 'Storage.'

'Storage? Right, do you work somewhere local?' Jacob chirped, blunt in his efforts to size up Niles.

'Yes, but I don't just work … I own it; it's my company. Our central branch is local though we have expanded and also have numerous satellite sites.' The exaggerated tone continued. Niles seemed to reposition himself so that he had his back to Babcia. He seemed to want to promenade for the group, but not for her. I think she had him spooked.

'Mm-hmm.' Jacob mirrored Niles' behaviour as he crossed his arms and looked up at him. He seemed impressed by Niles' pitch. I imagine Jacob would approve of businessmen; it meant money; it meant smarts. It was an opportunity to associate with a form of power.

Niles continued at volume, 'Personal storage, all

sizes, we're expanding again at the moment, it's a lot of work, but we're good for it.'

Babcia was listening intently. I'd long ago realised that despite her age, her hearing was exceptional. 'Do not divide the skin while it is still on the bear,' she growled under her breath. A few turned to her. I'm sure they had no idea what she was talking about.

'I know this one,' I said to anyone who would listen, 'Don't celebrate too early; first you have to catch the bear. I like it; there's wisdom in that.' I absent-mindedly turned to share my thoughts with the closest person, an unlikely listener, Tabitha. 'Did you notice that Niles said *I* have my own company, not *we* have our own company.'

'Sorry, what?' Tabitha was busy watching as William and Dean discussed the placement of the fairy lights. Her particular attention was on William as he nego-tiated the rickety old ladder. He looked decidedly sceptical as he sized up the old specimen of a ladder, wondering whether he could trust it or not.

'It's not lost on me,' I continued to my deaf audi-ence. 'I wish it *was* his own company; I wish he hadn't dragged me down with him.'

Tabitha had perhaps now noticed that she was part of my conversation, and she'd decided that she really didn't care for it.

The group were moving into position to put up the lights. I heard Niles serve back a conversational gesture to Jacob. 'So, are you married? Kids?' Niles' voice was friendly, but I was sure he wouldn't have been interested in the answer.

'Married yes, kids no,' was Jacob's short reply.

'I imagine your wife enjoys coming to these gardens. I imagine the women chat away here more than actually garden,' said Niles.

'No, she doesn't come here. My wife is in very poor health.'

'My heartfelt condolences,' replied Niles smoothly.

'I have to care for her. Everyday … day in … day out.'

'That's a big responsibility.'

Niles was getting a more complex answer than I'm sure he'd bargained for. Quite a few pairs of eyes looked over, interested in Jacob's story. I personally hadn't heard him speak of his wife. Niles moved from one foot to another, looking around for an exit.

'It's a lot to ask of me, but it won't be forever.'

His comment left a silence in the room. I was sure I wasn't the only person wondering, *where's his compassion for his wife?*

*

In order to change the topic Niles turned to William, passing some fairy lights up to him. The lampposts had been designated as the base for many stretches of this festive sparkle. 'What's your work situation?' Niles asked.

Remy responded casually, 'My work situation? Well, you could say that it all started and ended with grid-locked traffic for me.'

'Sorry?' Niles shot back.

I was amused. I was sure that Niles was just looking for a one-word perfunctory answer from these people. Instead, he was getting true answers, true expressions of Jacob and Remy's lives. I muffled a nervous giggle.

Remy continued, 'Well, I've had a bit of a change in direction really. A bit of a wake-up call. I was stuck in gridlocked traffic. This is eighteen odd months ago … and I suddenly cracked. What was I doing? Spending my time living what I realised was someone else's life. I immediately wrote my resignation email there and then as I stood still in the traffic and sent it. I then drove directly to work and handed in my work car. I think you would call it absolute burn-out. It wasn't a break-down, but I was a hair's breadth from it.'

'Um … okay?'

'Working twelve to fourteen hour days, six days a week, of high pressure, always contactable. Money flowed but I'd just wake, work, come home, eat, sleep and repeat. And that was normal. I was told that this is what I should expect. This was life, my life; I was the picture of success apparently. How could that kind of life be successful? There was no success in living. It was utterly depressing. There was no life. I wasn't living. I was a robot, just chasing empty things. Money, status, career, success!'

'Yeah, tell me about long work hours,' interjected Niles.

'I didn't feel trapped,' continued Remy. 'I was trapped. So now I garden, which was the only thing that I wanted to do when I got off the hamster wheel. I'm in nature, I grow things, I nurture things, and my work feeds me right back.'

'Okay?'

'I met Babcia in my previous life.' Remy nodded to Babcia, and she returned his nod. 'I was Babcia's business advisor, finance, all that. I'm not now though, thank goodness. I'd much rather be her gardener.'

'Finance! A business advisor!'

This wouldn't have sat well for Niles at all. He'd have been much happier to relegate Remy to a lower status. The clincher for Niles would be Remy's business strength; this would've threatened Niles enormously.

'Yes, people have referred to it as a sea change. For my part, I think I just woke up and grew a backbone, found my voice and all that. I escaped someone else's life. My work was like a parasite sucking the life out of me.'

Niles began to twitch, looking around.

'Have you seen her gardens?' Remy asked him as he worked to secure the lights. 'Babcia's gardens? They're magnificent!' Remy was speaking freely, apparently unaware of his increasingly uncomfortable audience in Niles. 'It's a full-time job caring for them.'

'Them?' Niles asked, drawing himself back.

'Yes, there are many different sections to her garden; they are truly beautiful.' A wave of astonishment could be heard from the group. It was now apparent that there were many ears listening. To think that Babcia was wealthy enough to require a full-time gardener. No one really knew where Remy fit in to the picture until now. This lady sitting there in her stretched grey cardigan … wealthy? I'm sure this was a sizable shift in everyone's understanding of her.

There were fairy lights going up in many directions, criss-crossing the Birch Circle. Arms, hands, reaching in many directions, ladders being passed around. Babcia sat in the middle like a ringleader, barking orders, telling people what to put where and how. She shook her head angrily when people didn't understand exactly what she meant.

It was then that Margot decided to take the group in a different direction. 'So here we are, members of the Narcissus Gardening Club.' Margot was again working to keep a straight face as she said the club's name. 'We're all here for different reasons I think.' Margot liked to gently push the boundaries.

William shot a look of concern at Margot. I wondered what it meant.

We all turned to look at Margot.

'What are you saying, Marg?' Jacob said.

'Well firstly, please don't call me Marg, it's Margot.

Secondly, take you for example, and Dean in fact, you both seem more interested in being on the committee than being in the gardening plot. I'm interested in what's bought us all here.'

'Is there some subliminal lesson happening here, Margot?' Dean looked pleased with himself with his wanky words, although they didn't make much sense.

'I'm on the committee because Babcia asked me to be,' I said coming forward, 'and …' I smiled warmly to Babcia, 'she's very hard to say no to. That's not a very interesting story, however, the way I came to the Narcissus Garden Club is. I won a prize which was an allocated garden plot here and garden tools. I didn't even enter the draw. I have a fairly good guess which of my friends entered me though. My friend denies it of course, Alicia is a sweetheart, and she just knew that I needed some time away. Some tranquil time for myself.'

'And you ended up with this mob!' Tabitha sneered waving at the group.

'What about you, Tabitha? How did you come to join the committee?' questioned Margot as she turned toward Tabitha.

'I always do what I can for the community,' she said demurely.

As if passing a ball, Tabitha then turned her gaze toward Dean and we all followed her lead. Dean obliged and explained his presence. His official 'police report' tone returned. William looked astonished as he listened. 'As for your aforementioned question Margot, gardening has very good psychological effects on the individual … calming and grounding. I'm here because people said it would be good for me. They thought it would mellow me out.' He then broke from this official tone and in an attempt at humour said. 'This place might help me get in touch with my feminine side.'

I couldn't help myself. 'You mean create your feminine side'.

Dean, however, completely ignored me and continued, 'But don't worry, I haven't tripped and fallen into some feelings. If I did, I'd just brush that shit off.'

I gritted my teeth.

Dean continued, 'I know I come across as intimidating. Even my ex used to refer to me as a scary wolf.' Dean was clearly proud of his last comment. I groaned within myself, listening to his self-important slobber. This guy was just off on tangents.

Without skipping a beat, Margot swiftly and firmly replied, 'Don't worry, Dean; you don't come across as intimidating … not at all … you come across as scared.'

I nearly choked, trying to hold back my laughter. His expression was priceless.

To my surprise William interjected with a question for Dean, asking if he had ever been in the police force or the military. I'd wondered how Dean's official carry-on would be received by someone who was apparently actually official. This all seemed lost on Dean. Of course, he didn't know that William was here in a work capacity – whatever that was.

Dean replied, 'I was in the police force at one point in my life, yes.'

'Previously? For how long?' asked William directly.

'Six months.' But that was where the information stopped. I was sure that I wasn't the only one wondering why.

Dean stared at Margot. 'What about you? You have everyone else's story; why are you here? You must be part of this proletarian mass.'

I remembered then that Margot had once said to me, 'Dean's just trying to be an intellectual wanker, but he's not even pulling that off!' I just felt tired when I was around him.

'I truly love these gardens,' Margot said. 'They're a joy. Happy to help in their care'.

'Don't give me that crap. That literati crap,' he growled. 'All this happy, skipping through the fields bullshit. I never trust someone who's all shiny.' I was left baffled. Literati? Did he know what half his words meant?

'Well, there we agree, Dean,' Margot said. 'Actually, that is something that I find in your favour. You don't pretend to be Prince Charming. You might pretend a few other things, but not charm.'

By Dean's confused expression I was sure he was trying to decide if he'd just been complimented or insulted. Clearly, he decided to take it as an insult as he said, 'Well then, I'm just a lost cause, aren't I? A waste of space; clearly I can't get anything right.'

'And that, ladies and gentlemen, is a deflection.' Margot made a large, bowing gesture as she stepped back, arms spread out. 'Well done.'

I actually felt for Dean, but only for a moment.

Margot continued, 'A deflection is a generalised comment that is too extreme in nature for me to agree with, a victim statement if you will, designed for me to feel obliged to reassure him of the opposite. We would then find that the conversation becomes about how he's in fact wonderful in many ways.' Looking around the room, Margot was now addressing the broader group. 'Can anyone tell me what we're actually talking about? I've quite lost the topic, and this is the very goal of deflection. Moving swiftly from the topic at hand to their *I'm a victim* statements. *I'm just a terrible wife, husband, parent, employee, son, daughter. I can't get anything right ... Are you trying to upset me with these things you're saying?* These are all age-old defences. Age-old and effective forms of deflection.'

Dean truly had no idea of who he was up against if he was going to try his bag of manipulative tricks on Margot. Margot seemed immune from needing to be liked. And Dean was but a small fly.

'Dean, do you have reception here?' For the second time tonight William stepped in to diffuse the stifling tension that now hung between the players in the Birch Circle.

'Sorry?' Dean slowly turned toward William; he seemed confused.

'I'm having trouble with my phone. Are you getting reception?' With this, the two men engaged in distracting conversation. Now that the ruck was broken and ease had returned to our green room, I noticed Tabitha eyeing Margot with particular interest.

CHAPTER IV

'Babcia, are you happy with the lights?' Remy asked as the group took his lead, stepping back to look at the overall effect. One by one, he was turning them all on. There was a tapestry of lights above us, dancing in the breeze to lovely effect. This ceiling of delicate lights accentuated the shape of the Birch Circle. It looked like a miniature, festival stadium. Babcia was strangely quiet. A tiny smile spread across her face. This was important to her. Our circus tonight was important to her.

It seemed that the party preparations were moving much too slowly for Margot, however. I also felt like we needed to get a move on, or we'd be here all night. 'Remy, help me with these; let's whip them up as well before there's a fuss.'

Margot and I had seen him lug some red Chinese lanterns from his car earlier; we all knew they had to go up before Babcia would declare the party started. Between them, Margot and Remy were swiftly organising the lanterns into sections to hang between the lights that framed the Birch Circle.

They were then joined by other members. We all worked surprisingly well. There was definitely a sense of camaraderie growing. The night was absurd. The co-workers would soon be the special guests. Margot seemed lost in thought, her concentration intense. She stepped back. The rest of us had the task in hand.

Remy also stepped away from the group, and I heard him ask, 'You're not here, Margot. Where are you?'

'Hi?'

'Care to share your thoughts?'

'Very random thoughts,' Margot replied, distance in her voice.

'Sounds good,' encouraged Remy.

'They're a bit deep, I'm afraid.'

'More the better.'

'Well,' Margot took a moment, 'I'm actually wondering, do we ever really become adults? I look around me and I see most of us stuck in some childish form. Some childish way.' She smiled gently.

'At least this group are past the toilet-training stage!' Remy joked.

'That's true,' Margot said, grinning back, 'but I don't just mean this group. I mean the world. Some of us are stuck at the ignorant, self-absorbed, tantrum stage, some in childish, poor self-care stage, some in sulking behaviour where we expect the other person to know our mind, or we expect the world and success to come to us.'

'Mm-hmm, yeah I see that,' replied Remy.

'And, also … why do we only get stuck on the ugly side of childhood, not the beautiful side?' These words were said with such delicacy, such sincerity.

'So true.'

'We're scared of our own shadow … change … new kids on the block. Our heads torture us with our own personal bogey man of self-doubt … But we lose touch with where we got it right as kids,' Margot continued in an exasperated tone. 'Their joy, their playfulness, their wide-eyed wonder of the world, nature, all the micro moments that widen their minds. It's that word … awe. Living in awe.'

Her words clearly resonated with Remy. She had his full attention. He asked, 'Do you live in awe, Margot?'

'Far from it,' she answered, 'but I try to … there was this one time that really woke me up, that kind of forced my eyes open.'

'Yeah?'

'Well, Remy … your world changed with being in a gridlock. For me, I actually had an epiphany with butterflies!'

A broad smile splashed over Remy's face. 'Of course you did, Margot!' He seemed as enthusiastic as I was to hear this one.

'My boys and I were driving one day, just down a local street. We were on the way somewhere … nowhere urgent … nothing interesting.'

'Your boys, Finley and Henry, right?'

Margot nodded. 'So we're driving along and then to our absolute surprise, we drove through an extraordinary storm of butterflies. A storm … of butterflies … The air was thick with butterflies. Thousands upon thousands of them, in one thick blanket. A wonderful swarm of red butterflies. The swarm was so intense; you couldn't see through them. You couldn't see where the butterflies began or ended. It was truly beautiful. It felt … it felt miraculous.'

Again, as was the nature of the night, given our close proximity, there was a general hush in the group. Many ears were attuned.

Margot, was speaking only to Remy and seemed to pay no heed to the other ears, 'I was worried about hitting them with my car, of course, and hurting them, so I slowed down, right down, and then kept on my way. I was so impressed by what we saw.'

'That's pretty special, Margot. You would've loved it. But, I don't get your point.' I could picture Margot in this setting. Of course this would happen to her.

'Well, here's the thing,' emphasised Margot. 'It wasn't until afterwards when I spoke to someone … some months later, that I really woke up.'

'To what?'

'This person I was speaking to had travelled to the Amazon forest and went to great lengths, spent a fortune, trekked impressively, faced dangers even … to see this very thing, a massive swarm of butterflies. It was then that I realised what an idiot I'd been. Why didn't I stop the car Remy … why didn't we get out? Why didn't I stop my unimportant monotony of life and truly take in this rare experience? This could easily have been a once-in-a-lifetime experience. But I didn't. It would've been extraordinary. But I was too busy going where I was going, doing what I was doing, busy being busy.' Margot was very still and quiet as she spoke.

'I swore from that moment on, I'd get off the ferris wheel. I'd get out of the damned car, put my feet on the ground, feel the soil, open my eyes, and absolutely absorb beauty as it came my way. What's the point of being in the cinema if you don't watch the screen? We're talking here about perhaps the whole point of living.' Her voice was building. 'It's huge, Remy. It's about actually experiencing our lives, and I have worked to do this ever since. And you know what, it's like I've gone from being colour-blind to seeing in full colour. I now experience extraordinary joy from so much around me. Stupid things, amazing things, simple things, beautiful things. I still get it wrong a lot of the time. A lot. I still miss things. But I'm getting better at it, and that's what matters. I want to suck the marrow out of life, and I won't apologise for it or be subtle about it. I don't have my eyes closed any more. Not often anyway.'

'Well, I knew you'd have something quality or odd

going on in that head of yours,' Remy said, laughing. 'I'm not disappointed!'

'We both got out of the grid lock.'

'Yep!'

'It can be a dangerous question to ask what I'm thinking.' Margot smiled, now playful again. She softened so that only Remy and I could hear. 'There are many ears here. I wonder how many of them followed that?'

'Well, I hope many. A good dose of this would do them well. It really should be just common sense, but it's not,' said Remy.

'No … sadly, it's not,' she agreed. 'I often find myself watching people walking along with their eyes shut. Not looking, not *really* looking, or smelling, or tasting, or touching, or hearing. So why be here if you're not actually here. And with our cameras on our phones now! It seems it can be more about getting the perfect shot to impress others, rather than actually being in the experience.' She paused and looked at him apologetically. 'I'm sorry; I don't mean to get all preachy.'

'Preach away. I'm all ears. I'm a convert. Proud of it!'

*

Dean had been listening to Margot and Remy's conversation. It seemed that he wanted to wrestle with them, to show that he could intellectually join them. 'To progress our earlier conversation, Margot, about narcissistic people,' he butted in. 'It's just that they're very confident that's all. What's wrong with that?' How he made a link between these topics was lost on me.

The others came over to admire the finished lantern effect. There seemed to be no private conversations tonight. Margot looked irritated; her fingernails clawed gently on her throat. Two irritated people having a conversation; the opposite of what I wanted tonight. Many ears listened with interest.

'But they're not confident at all Dean; that's the point. That's the problem. That's the enormous problem.'

'Come on, really?' Dean was trying to sound powerful, but he wasn't pulling it off. I heard a touch of fear in his voice. Fear that polluted his façade. Fear that I'm sure Margot was about to crystalise.

Margot released a breath and entered the ring again. She spoke slowly, with a slightly patronising tone. 'Dean, people with Narcissistic Personality Disorder are super insecure; that is *why* they're all about themselves, that is *why* they try to have control, that is *why* they're so self-consumed and they don't take into account other people's needs or celebrate other people's strengths.'

'Makes sense,' piped in Jacob, trying to sound knowing.

'If say … hypothetically … you came along with a massive syringe and gave them a sizeable shot of confidence and authentic self-worth, I'd argue that they wouldn't be narcissistic anymore. They would feel fuelled up and be able to be aware of others and generous toward others. They wouldn't have a need for drama and control over others because they would feel calm within themselves.'

I wondered whether the narcissist label had been flung at Dean more than once. His eyes flickered from Margot to the host of figures that stood amongst us.

His agitation was clearly not a concern for Margot. She continued, 'They're like a bear with a sore tooth; they're in pain, so they're all about themselves. What's really, really sad is that they can't be truly happy. It's only when you know how to love others or love something bigger and more important than yourself, and to give with love, that you can be truly happy. Everything else is shallow and slips away.'

Dean seemed determined to deflect and twist this information. 'So, are you saying that they can't help it? That we should feel sorry for them?'

Margot didn't skip a beat. 'For the second time tonight, no that's not the case. As I said before, that's where the real harm comes in. They're usually capable of being on very good behaviour with people who are not close to them. In public they're often Mr or Mrs Charm, while at home when there are no eyes on them, they can be dominant, controlling, manipulative, criticising and antagonising. Gaslighting is the latest term. This proves that they have self-control when they choose to use it … when it's their priority. They actually let themselves misbehave with their close family. They have choice. It's their motivation, their intention, to be hurtful … harmful to their close people.'

I shot a wary look at Niles. *Can he see himself in Margot's description? Does he even care?*

Margot was bringing things to a close. 'So should you feel sorry for them? No, actually, they need to be held accountable for their actions and the impact on others. Should we have compassion for them? Absolutely!' Margot emphasised this point. 'While you hold them accountable for continuing to dig their own hole and bringing others down with them, you can also feel compassion for them and their world they keep destroying. It's ultimately a lose-lose for everyone whenever someone is tied up with someone with Narcissistic Personality Disorder. The ultimate loser in all of this, however, is the person with Narcissistic PD. I'd argue that because their value system is so off-track and corrupted, they can't experience genuine inner peace, connection with others and happiness. If you can't give from your heart and love, how can you be happy?'

Jacob puffed up his chest and piped in again. 'So that's why there's such a high divorce rate? I'm married. I can't understand why people can't just get it together.'

'What are you talking about, Jacob?' Margot snapped at him. I'm sure that I jumped. She was losing patience. Margot turned her attention from Dean directly to Jacob, her voice firm. 'You're talking about two different groups of people here, Jacob. You have no idea of what you're talking about. Usual divorce is because of relationship breakdown, conflict areas, or people growing apart from each other. But with Narcissistic PD, there's poison in the fundamental ingredients … in the relationship foundations. Any prospect of a healthy relationship is dead in the water here. You've got no chance.'

'That's what I said,' chimed in a defensive Jacob.

Margot ignored him and continued her point. 'In my experience you can't work with people who have Narcissistic PD to have a healthy outcome. They don't work to build … to resolve … to take ownership … to care. Their goal is to erode and control. So, if health is what you want … escape is your only option. This isn't about relationship issues; this is fundamentally extreme dysfunction within an individual.'

'So, they're controlling arseholes then,' said Tabitha.

'I wish it was that simple, but no, this isn't about just being controlling and dominating. Another key factor to NPD is their manipulation and their false mask to the world. It's not just being controlling, selfish and entitled. That's just a person behaving badly. The call card for people with Narcissistic PD is their psychological abuse and belittling of the other person's voice and self-worth.'

This conversation seemed to never end for poor Margot. Surely, she'd reached her limit. Surely, she wanted to down tools and not be a psychologist tonight. However, I inadvertently kept the topic's momentum going with my genuine question. 'So how do you deal with the manipulation?' I asked quietly. My question fortunately conjured a warm smile from Margot. This was an earnest, personal question, one that I'd have asked with no other ears present.

'You know, Anna, it's pretty un-Australian of me to say this … but I have pretty high verbal intelligence.'

'Of course you do,' I said in an instant.

'Having a high verbal IQ is key to my job. I'm in the talking sciences you could say. It's my professional world. But you know what … even I wouldn't be able to out argue someone with Narcissistic PD and achieve a constructive outcome. I can hold them off, but that's it.'

I felt like my world suddenly came into crisp focus. 'Really?' If Margot couldn't fix this, how the hell could I? I was kidding myself if I thought I could make my broken situation with Niles salvageable.

'Absolutely. You see, they don't play by the rules; they're not following facts or logic. Everything is just flipped and carried out at such high speed that you can't pin down the argument. It's like trying to navigate an ever-changing labyrinth.'

'So, what then?' I asked listening to every syllable. Margot wasn't giving me any hope, but she was giving me clarity. This was surreal. I was talking hypothetically, but Margot, myself and for sure Niles all knew

I was speaking about my home life. All in front of the group. I was running an autopsy while the patient … Niles … stood in front of me.

'Just don't enter into it; don't enter the conversational labyrinth. Don't engage.' Margot was deadpan in her answer.

She paused. 'Because you know, in truth, I think you have to ask yourself the question, *what is the point? What is the point* in trying to build a bridge of mutual understanding if the other person is actively burning this bridge down from their side? There's no good outcome here. And often to win the debate they just go primal and work to intimidate and criticise you, to psychologically abuse you. So why would you get into the ring with that? Just don't engage. Get out of there. Be with safe people. Full stop.'

Margot wrapped up, 'But if you absolutely do have to engage, the most important key is this: don't accept the premise of the question. I'll say it again, don't accept the premise of the question. When they lead you off to hell knows where, don't follow. Determinedly stick to the one first question, or important conversation topic at hand. The primary issue of the initial conversation. Don't be diverted, distracted, flipped, guilt-tripped, gaslit or taken in with the personal belittling.'

What a night this had become. Margot had simply come along to relax and enjoy the garden on this summer evening. And here she was, deep topics and questions fired at her – while her dear friend William circled a potential, mysterious crisis.

*

Babcia had been sitting away, listening to our conversation with interest. Margot nodded a conclusive gesture to the group and abruptly came to sit by her. I eagerly followed. In her lap, Babcia had a small string of table-decoration lights. She was trying to unravel them, but her fingers were pudgy, awkward and lacked dexterity. The delicacy of the lights made her hands look that much clumsier. I saw her struggling and wanted very much to help her, but a very determined Babcia wouldn't ask for help. I realised that with her poor close-up vision, this was an impossible task.

'Can you help me, Babcia?' I said with warmth. I received a gentle smile from Babcia in return. This was an extraordinary thing. I felt honoured, delighted in witnessing this rare, vulnerable underbelly of Babcia. I discreetly engineered it so that Babcia's job was to hold the string of untangled lights. This took the pressure off Babcia without her perhaps noticing. Margot sat back to relax. I smelled the aromas in the air. There was a timber smell that I couldn't place and the waft of the freshly cut grass that lay circling the perimeter of the Birch Circle. I breathed it in.

Babcia started chatting away to me almost immediately. 'You never can trust them.'

'Trust who?' I asked.

'Anyone.'

I found myself listening to the musicality of Babcia's accent. She spoke with low, whirling notes that would rhythmically build to a crescendo.

'Surely, it's not everyone that you can't trust,' I said.

'Ba, yes, some you can trust, but not many. You should never trust a Jack Horner. If you meet a Jack Horner, you do not open your door.' Her voice became guttural, a look of distaste across her face.

Margot looked reflective following this last, rather random statement. 'Sorry, you've lost me there, Babcia,' Margot asked. 'A Jack Horner?'

'Fe, yes never trust a Jack Horner,' Babcia was very matter of fact and stern in her reply, and that was that. These pearls of wisdom were lost on me. Then Babcia abruptly turned to Margot. 'Are you with someone?'

'With someone? Oh, *seeing* someone?' said Margot. 'Maybe.'

This suddenly irritated Babcia greatly. She barked, 'It is a yes or a no! Tis a simple question.' The queen of riddles didn't like riddles from others.

Margot calmly responded, 'Is it a simple question, Babcia? I find that if I say that I'm seeing someone, people get into a tizz wanting me to settle down and lock it in, and I'm not interested in what other people want.'

Babcia seemed to release, to exhale. She changed her

tune, I think she actually respected Margot because she couldn't intimidate her. 'You're right not to trust; you can be lured into believing someone is a fawn and then, snap they are a panther.'

Was Niles a panther? Was that what Babcia was saying?

Margot looked perplexed. 'Yes, you're right, Babcia; you need to know someone inside out, on a good day … bad day … stressed day and selfish day before you open your home and your heart. You need to know if they're a fawn or a panther, as you say. But for me, it's more that I'm content. I will in time I'm sure meet someone who makes my life even richer than it already is … but there's no rush. Meanwhile, I'm spoiled for company. And I never let them think that we're more than a lunch date. I keep their hope dampened right down.'

'You are wise,' said Babcia. 'You are wise … never trust, never trust.'

'Well, Babcia, if that's what you've taken from this little chat, that's all well and good, but really, that's not where my head's at.'

This whole conversation had me exhausted. Of course I was thinking about Niles … but I was sure that Babcia and Margot had more on their minds then my little domestic situation.

Gathering the small gems of light to decorate the table, I walked over to put them on a small bench nearby for safe-keeping. Tabitha sauntered over to me and, in an especially plum voice, said, 'Ignore any relationship advice from Babcia. She doesn't know anything about relationships.'

'Sorry?' I flicked her an irritated reply.

'Dear … sometimes you just have to work at your marriage. Niles seems lovely!'

I wondered briefly what Tabitha had overheard during our night's proceedings. What a presumptuous comment. Why had she even started this conversation? I shot her a cold look as I replied with a flurry of words, 'How can you have any opinion when you have no information, no clue, about what happens behind closed doors?'

'I'm just trying to help, dear,' said Tabitha, waving her hand dismissively.

I found myself gazing with a steely expression at Niles who was busy on the other side of the Birch Circle. 'That's an armchair opinion, Tabitha; you're not in the trenches here. Sure, he's lovely to the outside world. He's Prince Charming, and then when he gets home it's …' I stopped myself.

'But surely there are good things about him?' scoffed Tabitha. She wasn't actually listening to me of course, not actually hearing me.

'When the negatives are deal breakers, the positives just don't stand up! This hasn't happened overnight, Tabitha.'

Tabitha fidgeted with her brooch and shifted from

foot to foot, avoiding my eyes, 'Fine. Don't get yourself in a tizz, dear. I didn't mean to intrude.'

I, however, paid no attention to Tabitha's patronising attempt to exit. I wasn't going to let her off the hook that easily. 'But I've woken up. I can step away from the crash site now, and I can see it for what it is now. I don't have a clue how I'll do it … He has our finances all twisted up with legalities, tax and debt that he won't tell me about, but somehow I'll find a way.'

I wasn't actually talking to Tabitha anymore. I was more practising putting words to my thoughts. 'I don't care if the kids and I couch surf and eat off milk crates. We'll rebuild, and our future home will be safe and healthy. I should've done this years ago. I just feel horrible for the kids that this is their normal. They think it's normal for one parent to treat the other parent this way. They think this is a relationship. Well, no more … as soon as I find a way to tie up our affairs … it's done.'

Tabitha was actually trying to walk away as I pushed on. 'And you know … I actually feel so excited … I didn't realise … but I do … deliriously excited and scared all at the same time. I mean I feel weak, but I've also never felt this determined.'

Tabitha was now looking with agitation from one direction to another. Almost as if she wanted someone to step in or an exit hatch to materialise before her.

I looked at Tabitha and realised that I was speaking to an empty vessel. I could feel my blood pumping through me. I felt strangely proud of myself. I was practising having my voice and shutting down the idiot spectators who I was not going to give airtime to from now on. There would now be limits to my politeness. *Nice Anna* had just woken up. Or perhaps *Courageous Anna* had unfurled her strength. She would not put up with crap anymore. I felt a broad smile come over my face. My shoulders released. I sighed and walked off with pace, back to the larger party. I left Tabitha speechless, something I'm sure she'd rarely experienced.

*

Babcia had commanded us to retrieve our contributions for the party, so we all wandered off, each on different paths, to our cars. William went to the outer boundary of the gardens, reaching for his phone as he walked. I was sure I wasn't the only one glad to get away from the group, even Babcia's watchful eye.

'Hello again.' Remy calmly wandered up to Margot and I. We fell into step walking together. 'Good job on the decorations; they're very on-theme, very "Midsummer's Night"!'

'Yeah,' joked Margot. 'Clearly a very serious business!'

'You know, you're an odd one out here, Remy, did you realise?' Margot casually said. 'Anna, don't you agree?'

'What do you mean?' Remy asked for both of us.

Margot continued, 'Well, you're like a calm duck

surrounded by flapping ducks.'

'What?' he said laughing. 'Yeah … this place is often too much.'

There was a quiet pause until Remy turned to Margot again. 'What do you think of this circus?'

'Actually,' replied Margot, 'I can get quite bored by all this carry on. It's all very predictable. How often can you watch the same movie before you become bored? It is a bit like that for me.'

'Boring?' Remy seemed astonished. 'Actually, these Narc Club members always keep me on my toes.'

'But Remy,' Margot said, 'people like these folk are really patterns repeating. Predictable patterns. You just have to step out and notice.'

'Patterns?' asked Remy.

'Yeah…' Margot brushed a hanging branch out of her way as we walked. 'For example, we're about to get the food out, the hors d'oeuvres.'

'Yeah?'

'It's going to be egos at ten yards. Do they care about the food? No. They care about being right, showing off, about having the last word. What's more boring than that? Sad and boring.'

We continued to stroll together; we were in no hurry. We had taken a side exit from the Birch Circle and walked the long way around the gardens, out beyond the perimeter of the nuttery and The Hub. It was dark and beautiful. You could hear the crunch of the twigs and leaves under foot as we walked through the silence. It was wonderful to be surrounded by such quiet. Even if it was a mirage with suburbs encircling us just beyond the perimeter of trees, I felt immersed in nature.

Margot looked to Remy. 'Now, your question from before. Go!'

'Do you turn off?' Remy asked Margot. 'I bet you don't. I bet you read the room, read the people. I bet we're all just lambs to you.'

Margot scooped her hair up, tying it up in a messy bun to cool her neck. Shaking her head, she gently replied, 'Not at all, Remy. I'm not going around contemplating everyone around me with effort. But I must admit, just like an architect can't close their eyes to buildings they pass by, a decent psych can't turn off their knowledge, nor would they want to. They're handy life skills.'

'Fair.' Remy nodded. 'Humour me, how about here? Read something or someone in the room … in our Birch Circle.'

We were just now returning to the Birch Circle, with most people having also gathered their party contributions. We stood back a moment.

'Okay,' Margot looked around, 'let's take our fair maiden Tabitha. What do you observe?'

Remy looked quizzical. 'She's pretty obvious, isn't she? She's a want-to-be glamour puss. My favourite thing is how she actually keeps talking to an empty room … an actual empty room. How does she not notice? How can she be that consumed by herself?'

'Yes,' agreed Margot. 'She seems to need to fill every moment with words.'

'Incessant talk!' This clearly annoyed understated Remy.

'Yes, all true. But look at her heels. What do you see?'

'They're leopard-skin high heels ... bit excessive ... probably bought for the occasion ... but ... what about them?' I said, puzzled.

'Are they new?' Margot was playing now.

'Yes, they're brand-spanking new. They're perfect. I don't get it?' I said.

'Are they? Sneak a look at the soles.'

We stood together quietly, trying to be discreet as we looked around. In a short time, Tabitha put her knee on a chair as she reached to the centre of the table to correct Margot's arrangement of the roses.

'The tread? The tread on the sole of her heels is almost completely worn away,' exclaimed Remy.

This didn't make sense. The two parts of the shoe didn't match. The top of the shoe was perfectly new, the sole was very worn.

'Yes, sadly, my bet is our dear Tabitha has OCD, with part of her presentation being cleaning. She clearly cleans her shoes to within an inch of their life. I've noticed this about her many times. The confirming clue for me is that her hands are also routinely red and irritated, so I'd say that she's likely to be an obsessive hand washer as well. And have you noticed her brooch?'

Remy and I both nodded like compliant school children.

'How often does she wear that brooch?' Margot asked.

I jumped at this. 'Always … she always has it on.'

'Do you not think it's a strange thing that a woman always wears an elegant brooch like this when we see her here in her gardening clothes? There's a story there. A very significant story. Something to do with loss would be my guess. Shall I go on?'

'There's more?' Remy was clearly fascinated, as was I.

'Yes,' replied Margot in an *of course* kind of way. 'I think poor Tabitha is a closet smoker. I can hear it in her voice, but she doesn't have smoker mouth wrinkles, or tarred fingers, so I'm thinking that she's taken up smoking again more recently. It would be utterly bizarre for her to take up smoking in her sixties for the first time, especially with her desired image, so I'd confidently estimate that she smoked in her early life and has reached for this ghost of addiction again. Once a smoker, always a smoker in my experience. Cigarettes are always there waiting to trap you. She wouldn't be proud of smoking of course. It clashes with her image, so she hides it … poor thing.'

Remy looked utterly perplexed, as did I. 'I'm totally blown away, Margot,' he said. 'I don't know what to say. I must see the world as one dimensional compared to you. That was seriously impressive. I'd love to be you for a day!' Remy reconsidered. 'Or maybe I wouldn't. Is this a gift or a burden? I don't know which.'

Margot patted him on the shoulder. 'Wouldn't have it any other way, Remy. But you know what, we're having too much fun. I'd better do some work before I get into trouble.' I enjoyed her jest. The truth was, I think Margot very much enjoyed getting in trouble from Babcia.

CHAPTER V

Tabitha motioned to Niles to reach for her basket. He glanced around awkwardly but did as instructed and put the basket of food on the main dining table.

'What!' An alarmed blast came from Babcia. 'Are you trying to turn a cat around by its tail? What are you doing? You cannot put the food on the table until we have laid the tablecloth!'

Niles' jaw and fists clenched. He moved his jaw from side to side. I'd seen this tell from him many times. To be spoken to like that again by Babcia was taking him beyond his boiling point. To be honest, Babcia's hostility toward Niles that night was starting to puzzle me. I mean, it was normal for her to be abrasive, but she wasn't a bully. For some reason, she'd really taken an aggressive dislike to Niles right from the start, and I couldn't work out why. It wasn't as if he'd shown her anything but courtesy.

Tabitha hummed and smiled smugly as she withdrew a perfectly ironed, white tablecloth from the basket and laid it out with great ceremony. This was clearly an important ritual for the two women. A perfect, white tablecloth. Babcia gave a rare, pleased nod.

Margot's flowers were again placed on this white canvas. Tabitha then moved in on Babcia's territory as she barked orders, correcting everyone's contribution. Her pedantic directions for the placement of items was excruciating.

As I produced the punch bowl, Dean insisted on carrying the drinks around. When William offered to help, Dean refused with a firm frown and shake of his head. He somehow thought he was proving something by doing all of the lifting himself.

Jacob waddled up to us and produced a bottle of vodka. 'As you instructed,' he said with a slight, mocking bow to Babcia.

Babcia replied, 'That is ridiculous.' But she raised an eyebrow with interest to examine Jacob's offering. On studying the brand of vodka, she clearly approved as Jacob didn't receive a roasting.

'Is this for the punch then?' Jacob asked.

'Add a bit of punch to the punch!' I shared a very bad joke.

With that, Babcia barked yet another order, 'Not until we say *na zdrowie*! Only after our *kieliszek wódka* has been poured, would you dare to put wódka into a drink.'

Clearly the vodka was to be used for celebratory shots to officially open the Narcissus Gardening Club party. Only a drizzle would be left for the punch.

Jacob poured the shots of vodka, while Babcia issued a stern warning not to drink until later in the evening, when, under her direction, we would have our celebratory cheers. When that would be was anybody's guess. In a moment of awkwardness, we all found ourselves standing holding our plastic cups of vodka, lost as to what to do with them. It was almost comical. Then we unfroze and each of us found a surface to place our cups on until Babcia was ready to celebrate. Babcia instructed Dean to put her glass on the table directly behind her.

'Now, with the remainder, you can make your whatever … your punch, Anna,' Babcia instructed.

As if mixing a cauldron, I enthusiastically started combining the liquid ingredients. I was happy to immerse myself in this task.

'We're going to have a tropical, sparkling, vodka punch,' I declared. 'Perfect for this summer evening.' I'd put some thought and prior effort into this punch. I didn't know it would include a drop of vodka, but that worked too. I added sliced limes, strawberries, lychees, soda water, pineapple juice and tropical juice.

As I was adding passionfruit and pineapple icebergs, I watched Margot again sit by Babcia.

'*Na zdrowie?*' said Margot.

I liked Babcia's surprise. She was so expressive, showing her astonishment with her whole body.

Babcia's arms spread out to either side like a baby's startle response.

'I imagine it means to cheer to good health, wishing people well, success?' Margot asked.

'Ba,' replied Babcia in agreement. She was tilting her head back, looking down the line of her button nose at Margot, a strange frown of interest on her face. 'It is not a celebration without wódki.'

'We all have our ways! I personally like to celebrate with a Hemingway Daiquiri!'

With that, Babcia's truce of neutrality toward Margot snapped back to an aggravated splutter, 'Ala!' Margot had returned to being someone who irritated her.

I just knew that Margot would be enjoying this little clash with Babcia. Babcia was like an exaggerated character in a book, not necessarily an enjoyable one, but definitely one who bought personality to the world. Margot had told me that she'd been reading up on the Polish proverbs and sayings that we frequently heard coming from Babcia's pursed lips. Margot had made it a pastime to be able to try to interpret Babcia's foreboding rants. While Babcia's tongue ties were mostly lost on me, it had become sport for Margot.

Margot would've looked to our evening with the hope of hearing more of Babcia's eccentric phrases of wisdom, and she wouldn't have been disappointed. As for Babcia, I'm sure that for her to lose her ability to shock and undermine with her piercing words would not be a welcome thing. Even if the words were understood and even when they were anticipated, Babcia's imposing and guttural delivery commanded shocked attention. You couldn't become immune to feeling the force of Babcia.

Jacob waltzed past me, then suddenly stopped in his tracks. 'I've just noticed,' he said, 'you've changed your hair colour, Anna. Weren't you blonde? I liked it the other way.' I don't know if Jacob thought this was a compliment.

I instinctively turned to Margot for guidance. My vulnerability had returned. I had no space for someone like Jacob tonight. My plan for the evening was to stay away from stress and keep Margot close. I was faking keeping it together.

'Anna, honey, Jacob is just jealous that he's not young and gorgeous,' Margot said.

Babcia piped in with enthusiasm, 'A pretty person looks pretty in everything.'

I didn't know how to take this either. I felt by default offended by Babcia.

'No,' Margot said, with a depth and calmness in voice. 'Babcia means a deep compliment.'

I automatically walked closer to Margot. When you feel like you are going underwater, you reach for your floatation device. I just didn't need this attention on me tonight. We stood next to each other, shoulder to shoulder, her facing the group, me facing away.

I whispered, 'You know, I feel clear and determined, but as frail as a feather tonight.'

'I know, beautiful.'

'I don't know if I should really be here tonight. It doesn't feel right. Everything doesn't feel right. I feel constantly startled. I feel like there's danger around me. It's stupid, I know.' I couldn't help it; I twisted, searching the space for Niles. Sure enough, he was glaring at me from across the table.

Margot almost whispered back, 'I can understand that, Anna. Beautiful, you're on the cusp of some pretty enormous steps at the moment. You've got a lot going on.'

I looked at her, waves of self-doubt washing over me. Sure, the end of my marriage was putting me on edge, but it was more than that. All those meaningful glances between Margot and her friend – what did they mean? They'd let something slip about crises and crime and *murder*. This sense of dread, was it all about Niles, or was it something more? I had a sudden urge to get out, get away from all these people.

Margot leaned even further toward me. 'Remember … you're going to make sure that you're only surrounded by people who deserve you, not hurt you.'

'So much for a night of escape!'

'You'll be okay. I've got you, beautiful.' She squeezed my hand. I squeezed her hand right back.

Babcia had somehow heard our words. How could an elderly woman have such good hearing? She looked to me with a tender expression, and then Margot. Feeling Margot's care, I felt a quietening within me. Babcia, however, confused me. Her softness. It was like watching steel chains melt seeing Babcia's tenderness spread over her face. Babcia was smiling at me, an unreserved, caring smile. It filled her face and altered her usual look completely. This startled and stirred me deeply. I was seeing something that I didn't understand. Someone I didn't know.

Babcia then leaned toward us. She quietly said, 'You and Niles go together like an ox and a carriage.'

I smiled awkwardly. What did this mean? Surely she didn't think that Niles and I went well together; surely she meant the opposite?

*

With the decorations, lighting, drinks and table setting prepared, Jacob walked to the group with great ceremony. With his chest puffed out even more than normal, he proudly presented his banner to the group. He had been assigned this task by Babcia and had clearly taken it very seriously. With William's help, he unrolled the hand-painted material sign. It read THE NARCISSUS GARDENING CLUB BIENNIAL PARTY.

'You idiot!' Babcia launched herself like a vulture to her prey, 'You did me a bear's service!'

'Excuse me?' replied a very indignant Jacob. 'You asked me to make a sign and I made a sign.' With a hostile, shrill yell he finished with, '*You* should be grateful.'

Babcia from deep in her throat bellowed back, 'Ala! It is biannual, not biennial you fool. We're not having these every two years. The committee decided to have this party twice a year, biannually!' She waved her arms in the air. She barked at him, 'From the rain, straight under the drainpipe!'

'Well, there you go,' Margot jumped in, 'I didn't know that, Babcia! Biannual and biennial, what is it? Twice a year or every second year? Huh, well there you go.' Whether Margot was softening the blow for Jacob or genuinely interested I didn't know.

Dean spoke up, 'Actually Babcia, you can be assured that as per committee meeting notes, *you* decided, not the committee, that it would be twice yearly. I think *you* will find it wasn't a unanimous vote. Your recollection is amiss, I'm afraid.'

With a dismissive, flicking gesture, Babcia scoffed at Dean, 'The drowning man catches at a razor blade.' Babcia was on fire tonight.

I reached for Remy as he passed by. 'Why do her Babciaisms always have an edge of despair?' Remy smiled. There was a macabre quality to Babcia's riddles, no doubt. But strangely there was also a lot of heart and a precision in her delivery.

And with that, Babcia returned her attention to her

first victim; she wasn't done yet. To Jacob she said, 'Your help is as necessary as a hole in the bridge!'

I'd been so absorbed by the commotion, that I hadn't noticed that Niles had come to stand beside me. As if in mid-sentence he said, 'But you said that she has bad vision, so how does she see that?'

I shuddered. I didn't want him in my space. I'd separated from him in my mind, now I needed to separate from him physically.

Margot stepped in as she saw my rigid reaction. She said, 'Up close, Babcia can't see well. She won't admit it. But she's like a hawk on mid to long distance. How else do you think she examines everyone's gardens pedantically? She circles from a distance.'

Remy, in his gentle way, walked toward Jacob and suggested that the change to the sign could be easily done. As the two men walked toward the shed, Babcia continued to bark orders at them from her chair. Jacob looked so wretched in his humiliation, I almost felt sorry for him.

'So … let me see if I've got this right? The people preparing the party are the guests of the party, and you're giving yourselves a banner! That's utterly absurd,' Niles said.

Again, Margot spoke for me, 'Yes, it is. True Babcia style. We celebrate the absurd around here. Welcome to the Narcissus Gardening Club!'

Niles got the hint. I wasn't going to engage with him.

Perhaps he was worried that others would notice because he strolled away. I watched as he wandered up to Dean. Niles decided to throw Dean a bone and sound like he cared. 'Hey, I'm sorry you're having such a rough time with your ex. All that would drag you down,' he said.

Dean frowned, shaking his head, and deflected, 'No, I'm fine, I'm on top of it. She's just a misandrist.'

'Oh, a what?' Niles paused. 'Women can be hard work! They don't make sense a lot of the time.'

Dean looked at Niles blankly. They both just stood there for an awkward moment.

I wasn't the only one to have my interest piqued by this nearby conversation.

Babcia chortled under her breath, 'A wolf carried away many a time, was eventually carried away itself.'

Margot was nodding.

'What?' I asked her.

'I know this one,' Margot said. 'Babcia can nail it sometimes.'

'I don't follow.'

She explained for me, 'There is an end to all ruthless action. No matter how powerful a person seems at the time, their end comes inevitably.'

'Who's she talking about?' I asked.

'That's the delicious part. I don't know. There's more than one person here who needs a good dose of natural justice.'

*

There was a loud clapping of hands. '*Jedzenie*, the party is ready. Now we shall all enjoy the gardens by night. I have scheduled a stroll in the gardens before we eat. We shall reconvene for our party in twenty minutes,' declared Babcia. She ordered her soldiers forward. As random as this suggestion was, we all jumped to it, as the last person to disband, to leave the circle, would've been left there with Babcia's glare. Anything to avoid her launching into one of her jarring attacks. I often wondered if not understanding Babcia's insults made them less offensive. But her tone was so clearly a spitting of words, you really received the assault either way. Or, more accurately, *other* people received the assault. Her mercy toward me was a mystery. But her valued regard for Remy was clear. He was an ally. He was behind the bunker wall with her.

Margot and William turned to walk around the outside of the gardens toward The Hub, and I hurried to join them. Niles had looked at me, and I wasn't convinced that he wouldn't follow us, but the shield of William and Margot seemed to be working.

Margot was clearly glad for a moment with William. 'So, my dear friend, what do you make of all of this?' I gave them a bit of distance to talk together.

William looked at Margot. 'Well, I've never had a night like this one, that's for sure. The setting is really something, and the people are far from bland.'

'A group of misfits that don't fit together!'

'Yes,' William said laughing.

Margot reached for his arm and turned him toward her. There was a seriousness in her voice, 'But … I have a sense that drama is being courted.'

'What … bit dramatic, Margot … Explain?' William lowered his eyes to hers.

'I can't put my finger on it. I sense that something is going to give. We may joke … but in truth, I believe that there are all of these pieces here to different puzzles … and somehow … somehow they work in together.'

'Margot?' William dropped his tone even further. 'I don't like hearing this … for you of all people to say this. It's like getting an ominous reading. Dread …'

Margot just continued. She didn't seem to acknowledge William's response. 'There's a stirring here; it feels like pressure is building from the inside out, if that makes sense.'

'No … that doesn't make sense at all, Margot.'

They stopped walking. I stopped. 'A reckoning of sorts.' I'd never heard this sombre voice from Margot before. William was taking her very seriously; his head was lowered to hers, his eyes flashed alarm. I felt a shiver, a twitch through my shoulders.

'Margot, this is pretty foreboding. What are you proposing? You're a bit of a weather forecaster with this sort of thing … I wish I could just brush this off.'

It was Margot's turn to sound surprised. She gently put her hand on his shoulder, picking off some specks of something. 'A forecaster?'

As he explained, she reached out her hand to me. I stepped toward them, happy to join.

William continued, 'You know those people who can look at the clear sky and read when there is a subtle change in atmosphere that no one else can see or sense … they can predict an approaching storm. That's you, Margot. Except you can predict the storm of people's making.' A pensive frown came over his face. 'Please be wrong,' were his flat, serious words.

'I'll try.' Margot hesitated a smile. 'I wish I could just say that I feel it in my feathers, but there are too many facts to ignore. I'm very concerned.'

I squeezed Margot's hand without meaning to. I'd been feeling a sense of danger throughout the night myself. My body was jumpy. I was at tipping point. To hear this solemn seriousness from Margot, it was like having my body's prophecy come true.

William was now blatantly staring at her. I wondered what this all meant to him. I knew that Margot worked a lot with the police as a psychology consultant for tricky cases. Perhaps this was how Margot first met William if indeed he was a police officer. This must have been what Margot was referring to earlier in the garden when she had said that she didn't want to be in work mode here with William tonight. As the picture was coming together, it was not relief that I felt; it was heightened fear. Fear on top of fear. Was that even possible?

'Pieces, pieces … what facts are you referring to, Margot?' William asked.

'It's more of a picture forming but there are a few pieces that still don't make sense.'

This seemed to be all that Margot was going to share. Despite William continuing to try to draw her out, she shared no more.

*

We returned to overhear the tail end of some sort of stoush between Babcia and Tabitha. 'I've mine here in my basket,' Tabitha snapped back to Babcia.

We instinctively hung back not entering through the pathway of trees. We stood in the darkness. We could see through the birch-tree trunks to the brightly lit inner pad of the Birch Circle. It was like a stage, lit up.

To my surprise, Babcia stood up. She evidently was set to go for a walk herself.

'Shall I come with you?' We heard Remy ask after her.

'Ćśś.' She waived a hand in the air as she walked away. He stood down.

There remained Remy and Tabitha alone. What we saw next was like a pantomime. Tabitha suddenly moved in close to Remy. She was swift. She stood directly in front of him, toe to toe, her chest touching his.

Remy stood there, startled. She slid her hand into his, and the other hand, firm, to his shoulder.

To my astonishment, Tabitha began to sing. Was it singing or humming? I wasn't sure. She was swaying from side to side. She was holding him to her. I'm sure in that moment she thought she was a flamenco dancer. A flush of embarrassment came over me. I felt embarrassed for him and surprisingly her. Even from this distance, I could see that Tabitha was enjoying herself; she had her seductive vixen face on. She was amazing. How could she believe that she was so desirable? Her understanding of men was so very simple and one dimensional; it was insulting. Reality had no voice here. I was torn as to what to do. I wanted to go in and extract him, but that might be even more embarrassing for him. I stood frozen in indecision. William and Margot also stood alongside me, three frozen figures.

Stiff as a plank, Remy leaned back away from her as far as his arms would reach. He looked desperate. Remy then abruptly unlocked himself from her. He spun around and walked out of the Birch Circle at great speed. Fortunately, he chose a path other than ours. He made no attempt at social pleasantries as he extracted himself. He was just in clear flight mode. He'd successfully disappeared.

William spoke for the three of us, as we walked again through the tunnel of trees to the Birch Circle. 'Unbelievable!'

We heard a triumphant sound from Tabitha; she was congratulating herself as she too left through another garden path. 'I'm just too much for him!'

'Yeah, mm-hmm, she's much too much for him,' I said. 'How can she flatter herself after that?'

Margot nodded with a sad tone. She seemed lost in thought. 'Why is Tabitha so determined to get at Remy?' she said. 'She normally carries on with men, but this, this is a whole new level … she's … she's a bit desperate … utterly determined. Why?'

Margot returned to her private thoughts.

*

The feast was to begin. On our white tablecloth there was now a smorgasbord of edible colour. I'd unfortunately brought an excess of food. I was a puppet for Babcia here, platter upon platter of deli-prepared delights. Margot presented a plate of cheeses that she clearly planned to stand by and enjoy. Tabitha proudly laid out her mini tartes flambées, while Jacob plonked his jar of olives on the table. There was no suggestion of how he'd serve them; you clearly had to just dive into the jar itself. Dean also seemed pleased with himself as he produced a plastic plate to put his packet of savoury snack biscuits onto.

Babcia glared at the fingers that crept forward during the setting up, reaching for a little sample here or there.

Standing amongst us, Tabitha was like a dark cloud. She flicked her attention between Remy and Babcia. She reminded me of when you can see the first hint of a dog about to growl, when there is a twitch movement of the lip. I wondered if it was her dance rejection from Remy that churned in her mind. She wasn't feeling embarrassed or self-conscious; there were no emotions in those directions. She was angry. It was almost a tantrum huff. Tabitha beckoned Jacob to join her at the back of the group. He fumbled slightly toward her, eyebrows raised.

'And what about that hired hand?' spat Tabitha as she gestured toward Remy.

I spun around, happy to let her know that I was in ear shot.

Jacob and Tabitha ignored me and leaned into each other to continue the conversation. They were both salivating with bitchy gossip.

'Yeah, what's his story anyway?' sneered Jacob.

I hadn't stepped in earlier and felt terrible for it. This was my chance. I interjected, 'Why does he need a story? Perhaps he's just a nice guy. Nice people are around, you know. Nice, kind people …' Was this all that I could come up with? Pretty feeble.

Jacob just ignored me. 'Yeah, he's so quiet, eerily quiet. It's infuriating.'

I changed tack. 'Do you have to?' Again, no impact.

Tabitha continued, 'He's just always around, just there, you know, just there.'

Jacob was leaning back with his arms crossed. As if speaking with old-man wisdom he said, 'He has to be in it for something. And you know, it wouldn't be the first time that scandal hit her. You know Babcia's husband cheated on her, don't you? Her husband went back to her, but the affair still happened … that's a fact!' He seemed proud of this piece of gossip.

With an exaggerated hand gesture, Tabitha replied, 'I'm not interested in any gossip, but you can't blame the man for cheating on her. Who would want to be chained to that? The poor man, he could've escaped.'

I glanced from one of them to the other. They were incredible; they were heads of the same serpent. My efforts could not and would not have any effect on this pair, but I was glad I'd tried.

The queen flicked her hand toward the table. The food had all been placed; the festivities had begun. The staff had become the guests. There was an eager movement of chairs, everyone finding a spot to sit and relax. Once the nine members were all seated around this large, square table, it felt either intimate or claustrophobic, depending on your mindset.

I had skirted away from Niles and sat beside Babcia.

'Thanks for the food, Babcia,' I said.

She waved a dismissing hand. 'Tell me about your son and daughter,' she said. 'What are their hobbies?' I was happy to oblige. I didn't much like small talk either.

With effort not to look interested, William watched on as Babcia curiously delved into my world. She had many times wanted to know about my kids, not Niles, just our kids.

More curious still, Babcia was speaking quietly. 'It's good that they do sport … fresh air is good for them, good for their lungs … good for their bones.'

'It's tricky because they often have games at the same time in opposite directions,' I said.

'Why doesn't Niles take one of them?' she asked the logical question.

'Well, it's just not like that … *he's* not like that. Niles just looks after Niles. At the beginning of the sport season, he goes maybe to put on a good front, but then he drops away. There's nothing in it for him.' I was finding Babcia's strange tenderness disarming.

She reached for my arm. I felt her small, pudgy hands soft on my skin. She had sweet hands, with one simple band on her right ring finger; her hands would have many stories to tell. 'A Pole is wise after the harm's been done.'

I saw William sneak a grin. What? What did this mean? That wisdom comes after effort or … difficulty?

'Niles is in charm mode tonight; he's in public and he knows he's on his last thread. But just wait till tonight … when we get home.'

'Home?'

'Actually, Babcia, can I tell you something.' I felt brave.

'Hmm?'

'I'm not going home.'

Babcia smiled. 'You are not going home with him?'

I couldn't place what was happening. She was being so warm. A crack into her soul was gleaming through. I smiled back at Babcia and felt a genuine depth of support. My heart released. I felt strangely close to Babcia in that moment.

'Hope is the mother of the stupid,' she said strangely with a smile.

William shared my startled confusion. His eyes darted to me, concerned about the potential impact. William turned to Margot and whispered to her and with that Margot leaned around William to join us.

'Hope is the mother of the stupid?' Margot repeated more as a question. Babcia proudly smiled back at her, nodding slowly and knowingly.

'Yes,' I said. 'That's what Babcia just said.'

Babcia looked on proudly.

Margot by some miracle actually understood the meaning. She said, 'Babciaw …' Margot nodded toward her in appreciation, 'is the only person I've met who speaks through proverbs like they're usual language. I enjoy it so much. It's like a riddle that she keeps throwing at us, and it's our problem if we have no idea what she's talking about. It keeps life interesting and usually, she throws them at you as a harsh insight or a curse even … but not this time.'

We waited for Margot to continue, but Margot was

in no hurry, she was enjoying the moment. She gently went on, 'Do you know how exciting this is for me? Polish proverbs that I read up on, coming to life. They're just so humorous and cutting.' Margot's eyes sparkled.

'Another hobby!' William rolled his eyes back.

'And then I come along here and wait to hear which one Babcia serves up next. I get to hear it with Babcia's accent and everything. My favourite was a time when Babcia was sharing her opinion of people who cheat. She said, "*Co cialo lubi, to duszę zgubi …*" What likes the body will lose the soul. This is poetry to me.'

'But what about, "Hope is the mother of the stupid"?' I said. 'Where do I go with that … sounds horrible.' Babcia was still smiling fondly at me, holding my hand even.

Margot humoured me. 'This saying means that we don't just sit and hope. We don't wait idly for our situation to improve itself. It's our action, our hard work, that creates our future.'

Babcia nodded with approval toward Margot.

I still felt lost. Wanting to move the focus, I asked Babcia, 'Were you ever married, Babcia?'

Heads turned, with many interested eyes now on Babcia.

Margot winced.

'When it is your time, you have to go. *Tak*, I had my husband for fifty-nine years. Tomek was a kind man; we made a good team.'

This was a very personal answer, a rare opening of a personal door. She could've just said *yes*.

Babcia continued, 'You can get distracted; it doesn't mean that in your blood you are not loyal. As long as you are true in the end, that is all that matters. Old love does not corrode.'

'Do you have any children? Any other family?'

To my continued astonishment, Babcia obliged, 'I had one son.' She looked at me meaningfully. 'He died when he was thirty-four. And I have one sister who I have also lost.'

'Oh, I'm sorry, she also died?' I reached for her arm gently.

'I have a younger sister, but I don't have a sister. She married a mercenary, a leech. This man Jack, he married her for her money, for my money. To protect her, I said that she would be cut off until she separated from him. She will then have money for every year of her life that she is not with him, every year that she is not with the leech.'

No one spoke. All waited to hear how the story ended. Babcia continued, her tone sombre and sad, 'But she has not left him.'

'How did you know this Jack was bad news?' I asked, 'Could you tell when you met him that he was just after her money, your money?'

'I haven't met him!' she said as if this was an absurd idea. 'Why would I meet such a man? A gold-digger, a leech! He has done this before, married women older than him. One he separated from and took an enormous share of her wealth, the other he married when she would soon die and she did, so he ended up a very rich man. But men like that don't hold onto their wealth, and my sister, almost twenty years his senior, was his next victim. But she wouldn't listen. Now she is old and ill, and I have not seen her for many, many years.'

'Babcia, that is so sad.' I looked intently at her; she was now not just Babcia, she was now a mother, a sister and a wife. The brazen facade of Babcia melted before me.

'How do you know she is ill?'

'I keep an eye on all those who matter to me.'

'Perhaps you could put the money aside and go see your sister?' I said, trying to be helpful.

'*Tfu*, this … this Jack has made it clear, unless I change my will back to include my sister, he will block me seeing her, and it seems that she agrees.'

I couldn't fathom that Babcia could have a defeated mindset, but here she was. I tried to move the conversation, 'So, you must be very successful for people to be after your money? That's a credit to you.'

'Ba, I grew up being told, "If you do not have what you like, like what you have," and I said *nie*, that is rubbish. Tomek and I dug ourselves free.'

'I'm sure you were a force to be reckoned with!' said Margot.

Babcia didn't so much as glance at her; she just kept her gaze on me. '*Raz na wozie, raz pod wozem.* Once on the wagon, once underneath it.' This wasn't enough, however, Babcia was on a roll. I was lost once again and felt mildly unsettled when she added, 'A success has many fathers; a failure is an orphan.'

'What's her name?' This question from Dean hung in the air, out of place.

'*Ala?*' grunted Babcia at him.

'Your sister's name?' pursued Dean with peculiar interest.

Babcia seemed irritated by this question, but she replied nevertheless, 'Marigold.'

'Marigold? A Pole called Marigold?' said Dean laughing.

Babcia stared coldly at him, yet she answered, 'It was a cold winter when my sister was born, and my parents looked for a flower from warmer places.'

'You were not named after a flower then?' Tabitha said with a prying, hostile tone. 'You could've been named after your favourite flower, the narcissus daffodil?'

Grins were either on clear display or were being held back with effort. Babcia didn't see the humour. She said in her thick, Polish accent, 'You are being ridiculous.' And the conversation was over.

As she reached for more cheese, Margot tried to ease the conversation back to a safer, more neutral topic. 'You know Babcia, I've been enjoying a pile of books on garden design, horticulture … companion planting. I often just look at the beautiful pictures, but they're so lovely to enjoy.'

'You are not a gardener!' snorted Babcia. And there it was, just when we had Babcia warming up, she reverted to her cutting self.

'Well, I enjoy my garden, I just love being on these grounds and … I'm a sucker for flowers.'

'*I cyprysy maja swoje kaprysy,*' Babcia cursed under her breath.

Margot smiled. 'So you're saying every fool is pleased with his own folly?'

Babcia spun in shock. Margot had understood her.

'Well done,' I said to her heartily. 'You've been studying up.' I was sure I wasn't the only one who shared this astonishment at Margot's dedication.

'I love a challenge,' said Margot grinning, with a wink to William.

Babcia blurted, 'But you do not grow flowers; your garden is a disgrace.'

'Yes,' Margot openly conceded, 'that's true; it's a tumble of weeds and dead plants at the moment.'

Babcia snorted, 'How can you call yourself a gardener?' She was back to her contemptuous throat contortions. This was beautifully ironic given that Babcia instructed and bossed Remy who did all of the garden work for her. Actually, many times I'd seen Remy gently going around what Babcia was telling him to do, quietly doing what he thought ought to be tended to.

Uninvited, Tabitha weighed in, 'I was once the *Garden Queen* and travelled on the head float of the city parade … they said I was the most beautiful flower princess.'

Jacob jumped in, 'A princess, hah, I'd believe that!'

'You were once … being the key words.' Dean almost spat.

This was completely ignored by Margot and Babcia as they continued.

'Babcia, I'm not disagreeing with you. But I like the idea of the garden. I've great plans and I plant them out beautifully, but I don't water, and I don't weed. All my enthusiasm and my plans end in shambles. But hey, I love the gardens. I love fresh-cut flowers from the garden; there is nothing like it. What makes us connect with true beauty more than flowers?'

Babcia gave a throaty scoff. 'You will never grow flowers.'

'Actually, that's probably true; apart from picking the wildflowers, I'm quite dependent on the lovely generosity of all the other clever gardeners. I always go home spoilt with gifts of flowers. Dahlias are my absolute favourite. They're so flamboyant and frivolous. I can't believe how often I'm blessed with a bunch of Dahlias! And my neighbour this afternoon gave me those beautiful roses that I came armed with tonight. Absolutely spoilt.'

Babcia was indignant as usual. 'A member of the Narcissus Gardening Club who cannot garden!' she scoffed.

Margot smiled warmly. Then Margot went too far, 'Perhaps I should grow some narcissus flowers; they self-propagate I hear. How could I go wrong?'

Babcia almost jumped out of her chair. '*Do not* mock the narcissus flower. I come from a proud heritage of the narcissus daffodil. We are proud of the narcissus. It is pure, triumphant beauty. Not for you to try to grow and kill.'

'Very wise, Babcia, very wise.' Margot then digressed. 'You know, I've great plans for a watering system. What do you think, Babcia?'

'That sounds about as helpful as incense to the dead. You will not turn it on!'

Margot nodded her head gently. 'You could be right again, Babcia. I'm all enthusiasm and a lost cause,' Margot said laughing.

'It is just a mess, atrocious, a disaster.' Babcia had not finished reprimanding Margot. She was almost spitting her words out now. Babcia clearly saw this as a failure. And I daresay that Babcia had not learned to take failure in her stride.

'Perhaps if Remy is ever lost for something to do, he could tinker in my garden?' Margot enjoyed provoking Babcia, like a mongoose playing with a cobra.

Babcia's hands gripped into her armrests, her

knuckles white with tension. 'How dare you ask anything of Remy? You have no right!'

Babcia, the poor thing, clearly had no ability to see when she was being mocked. She seemed to have one response and that was intense indignation.

Dean was strangely very interested in this conversation. 'But Babcia, you don't even get your hands dirty! You criticise everyone else's garden, but you don't get your hands dirty!'

With this Remy spoke up, 'I'm not a qualified gardener by any stretch, but Babcia has been kind enough to take me on as I'm learning.'

'He has enthusiasm and dedication, and he has my trust.' Babcia was almost bellowing. 'It is my right to garden even though I cannot bend and crawl on the dirt garden bed like I used to. If I can recruit someone to be my hands, so be it.'

'Well that just sounds intelligent,' Margot interjected.

Babcia suddenly gave her an approving nod, her hands releasing the strained grasp of her chair. She'd momentarily forgiven Margot. They were on the same team again. A truce until the next time.

A sudden, strong breeze blew amongst the circle of trees surrounding us. This hushed us. Nature now commanded centre stage. There was an eerie whistling through the trees. Sitting in a garden oasis under this night sky was such a rare thing. Here we were in a city and yet we were surrounded by silence, enclosing darkness and stars above. It was both beautiful yet menacing.

We relaxed for a moment and enjoyed the food. I had a moment to sit. To be.

*

'It is time for our *na zdrowie*!' declared Babcia with a thunderous bellow that startled me. Blank looks were soothed by Remy who motioned with his shot glass. It was time for our toast. The main meal was to commence, and the party was to be officially opened.

'Ahh,' was the general reply. There was a whir of commotion as most of the party needed to get up and locate their previously stowed shot of vodka.

Looking around the group, I tried to be helpful. 'Does everyone have their shot? No top-ups needed? No one snuck a sip or three?'

Dean was the only person to respond. 'Nup, the tide's still in.'

Everyone else just stood, drink in hand, diligently waiting for the command.

Glass held in the air, Babcia with a bellow declared, '*Na zdrowie.*'

'Cheers!'

We threw back our drinks. This was clearly a finely honed skill for Babcia. With one snap movement, she threw her vodka back down her throat.

For a split second, Babcia looked startled and

confused. She stared at me, eyes and mouth wide open. We locked eyes, but I couldn't read what was in hers. Then she let out a cry. I froze. What was happening?

Then the screaming started. It was brief, but it would stay in my mind forever. Agony and terror. She then started violently thrashing, desperately clawing at her throat.

Remy woke to action first. He rushed to her. William and I then launched toward her. Babcia clawed at the top of her blouse.

'What can we do?' we pleaded to each other.

We were rushing with no direction, lost as to how to help. Her eyes remained fixed on me. They were not of this world; they were horrifying to look into. They bulged out of their sockets with a mixture of agonising colour that I couldn't describe. Her colour was not human. Changing from purple to blue, she gasped for breath but the only movement around her mouth was froth projecting out. Although it felt in slow motion, as suddenly as it started, it ended. Her body stopped fighting; she went limp like a doll. She was released from her excruciating pain and fear. Babcia was gone.

CHAPTER VI

I fell back into who I don't know. My feet pedalled backwards; the space was spinning. I was searching for Niles. I locked my eyes on him.

'No! I can't. I can't,' I heard myself whimper. It was Niles who I was reeling away from. My heart felt larger than my chest, pounding; I couldn't breathe. I kept staring at him. When danger is circling, you must fix your eyes on it, keep the danger in your line of sight. But I couldn't keep alert to him. I was fading out; my focus dissolved from me. It was all moving, spinning; it was all getting dark. So dark. Then black.

I felt a waft of air over my face. I felt my head on a soft breast. I was being held.

'Water, William. Bring me some water,' I heard Margot say, her voice shaking.

I heard Jacob's voice. 'Here, have mine.'

My eyes could now slowly open. I was searching. Everything wasn't spinning now. It was coming into focus. There was a blue tinge to the trees above me …

the lanterns … the lights. I was cradled into Margot, held like a child, my body sprawled on the ground, one leg bent behind me. Margot was sitting holding my head and shoulders into her; her grip was firm. She was stroking my hair from my face. Stroking, stroking; I focussed on her fingertips.

'Ambulance … yes we need an ambulance!' Remy was yelling into a phone.

'What's she doing?' Jacob said. I felt him near me. I flinched.

'Yes, thank you. I think we're okay now,' Margot said, and Jacob stepped away.

Remy spoke in a firm clear voice. 'Yes, it used to be called the Seville Community Garden … yes the suburb is Seville.'

'Remy, I need to speak to them … hello.' William took charge of the phone. His voice faded out as he walked away.

Then my mind seemed to become alert. I bolted upright. That's what I'd intended to do at least, but my body didn't follow my command, instead I made a clumsy lurch forward. I searched the faces all mirroring the same expression of shock, until I found him. Standing back a little, Niles stood with his arms wrapped around himself. He was frowning intently at me.

'I can't … I can't,' I heard myself say again.

Margot drew my face to hers and stared into my eyes.

She looked lost herself. I could feel her fingertips along my jawline. 'Anna, listen to me, beautiful. You're going to be okay. You don't have to do anything.'

I gazed back at her; everything was foggy. The commotion around me was coming into focus. Babcia was lying on the ground. All I could see were her feet jutting out toward me. She lay like a rag doll flopped on the floor. Dean was working on her, compressing her chest, over and over and over. Her feet moved slightly with each compression. I felt a lurch inside me; it was only a matter of time before I vomited.

'Shouldn't you be doing mouth to mouth?' I heard Tabitha's shrill voice call out.

'No, don't be an idiot,' Dean said with laboured breath. 'She's been poisoned you stupid woman. Do you want me to die too! We don't do that now. Don't you know anything?'

'I'll step in. We'll take turns,' William said. He had returned, leaving Remy to take back the phone.

'I do this for a job, do you?' Dean said. 'I'm the first aid officer at work. You?'

I didn't hear William's reply as he took over from Dean.

'I'm going to stay with you'. Margot's voice drew my attention back to her. I heard her swallow.

'You don't understand,' I whispered.

'I think I do … this has tipped you over the edge. Fare enough.'

I nodded. There I was; Babcia had suddenly died a horrific death, and all my body could do was repel me from Niles.

'You don't have to do anything.' While Margot's voice was strong, her body shook ever so slightly.

With a little time, I was able to recover and gradually come to my feet. I clutched at Margot's hand. My gaze now returned to Babcia lying on the floor, William was working continually on her. One, two, three, four, one, two, three, four. I heard this over and over again. We all stood in a wide circle around her. The birch trees herding us in, stopping us from stepping back further. While William worked to put life back into her, Babcia was silent. Babcia was never silent. But it wasn't Babcia. It looked like a wax figure; her face was contorted and discoloured, and foam ran down it. One by one we looked away. It was too much.

There were no words.

Then Jacob for some reason turned his attention back to me. He blurted, 'What was that?'

'Yeah, I thought we had two down,' said Tabitha.

'Anna had a panic attack,' said Margot simply.

'A what?'

'A panic attack,' Margot said bluntly. 'Anna's … her body took over. It's a crisis reaction … she fainted. She'll be okay. She's going to be wiped out now. I'm just going to keep her with me.' Margot looked to me again. 'You'll be okay, Anna.' She kept her arm around me.

Niles needed to stay away from me. It was in that moment that the last thread snapped. I would never be near him again.

'Right,' William stood up, his body clearly cramped. He drew himself up to his full height as Dean took his turn working relentlessly on Babcia. Again and again, the compressions to her chest were rhythmic and, we all knew, useless. She was dead, but they just kept going. 'Now listen up, everyone. I know this has been a terrible shock for you all. It's not how I expected things to play out …'

'Expected?' Tabitha burst out. 'Of course not! What do you mean? What *did* you expect?'

'Hang on,' Jacob said. 'Just who are you, anyway?'

William took a deep breath. 'I was just about to tell you. I am Police Detective Sergeant Tarlington …'

'Police Detective?'

'Police?'

'What the—'

'Silence!' William spoke with a firmness that was entirely foreign to his previous, gentle way. 'I'll explain … everyone calm down. We're all going to move away from the scene. Margot, is there somewhere else?'

'There's another seating area, The Hub,' Margot said shakily. 'Follow me.'

'Thank you,' William said and took out his phone. 'You take everyone there while I wait with Dean for the ambulance. Stay together everyone; no one leaves.'

'I'm staying with Babcia.' Remy was resolute.

Our passage through the arbour seemed to take an eternity. I felt every heartbeat through my chest. Every footstep was an effort. Why was The Hub suddenly so far away?

'The police are on their way. The ambulance made good time though,' Remy said as he and Dean came to join us.

'Nothing?' Margot said more as a statement then a question.

'No, nothing could be done,' Remy said, nodding solemnly.

I found myself rushing to hug Remy. I squeezed him. I wiped the tears from his eyes. My appreciation toward him for staying with Babcia overwhelmed me. The true hero however was Dean, even though it was a futile attempt to find life in Babcia. I spun and walked toward him. My appreciation for Dean in that moment flowed out from me. Clearly this was not what Dean had in mind. He raised a hand at me and with a nod dismissed me from our fleeting exchange. He then beelined to one of the old bench seats. In his abrupt movement something floated down from his pocket to the path. The white of this slip of paper contrasted with the dark of the evening. I rushed to reach it for him. It was the least I could do. Remy, however, with an agile sweep, reached down and grabbed it before I could. A moment passed as he surveyed the content of the note. I waited for an explanation. But nothing.

'What is it?' I said. 'What's wrong?'

Remy barely acknowledged hearing me.

'Sorry, Anna,' Remy said flatly. These words were only cursory as he then walked at speed and sat in a corner seat. Such a small peculiar thing, but it was enough for my heart to again pound; my chest began rising higher with each breath. It was then that William made his entrance through the arbour.

'A moment please, everyone.' We all took his lead as he waved for us to come together.

'Babcia was pronounced dead by the ambulance. There was nothing we could do. Some police units will be here any moment, and the crime-investigation team shortly after.'

'But you are the police,' blurted Dean. He looked depleted.

'But-but are you saying you think she was murdered?' Tabitha rushed at him, her voice a high-pitched wail. William put out his hand. She stopped still.

'Well, we don't *know* at this stage. We need to consider all possible causes of death,' William said.

'Of course it was murder. That wasn't natural,' Dean said bluntly.

'We can't know this was a murder until we – the police – have investigated,' William said firmly.

'But you *are* the police,' Tabitha repeated Dean's sentiment.

Dean was shaking his head. 'So, are you telling me that they think that an eighty-something-year-old woman has passed away while having a lovely picnic in a local park and there is a policeman in attendance. They're going to think it was a stroke, or a heart attack, or an anaphylactic reaction or something ... some shit like that. They're not going to know what we've all just seen!'

William looked firmly at Dean.

'Is that their understanding?' Dean wasn't holding back his anger. 'Because if it is, then we're way down in their list of priorities. I wasn't in the police force for long, but I know this. They're just going to think that the old bat carked it. They're going to assume natural causes. They're going to think that you're here, so they have some police presence calming the situation down ... We're going to be zero priority. We're going to be here forever. Stuck here in this fucking garden!' William eyed him. 'With you lot!' Dean finished off.

Sirens could be heard in the distance. 'That's enough, Dean,' William said. 'The police are fully briefed on the situation. I'm not here by chance, Dean ... This is my investigation. I assure you this shall be treated as an utmost priority.' William had our full attention now. Tabitha's mouth dropped open. Dean took a step back, hands on his hips. Jacob was looking at each of us in turn with agitation. As for Remy, he was silent.

William spoke a bit softer now. 'I know this is all a shock. As I said, I will be heading up this investigation. Now you all just need to sit tight for the moment.'

Dean and Tabitha had dropped into their chairs. Niles, Jacob and Remy seemed to float down into their seats; there was a unity between us all. We were all shaken. I had the image of poor Babcia's face playing over and over again in my mind. How horrendously cruel. What was that? Now I didn't feel nature around us; I just felt shadows. I suddenly felt exposed. I wanted to go home, not my home I realised, but somewhere I could hide away and cry. Somewhere that I could have space to myself and just breathe, just process. I just felt numb.

'But what if one of us is next?' Tabitha launched again. On this rare occasion, I didn't think Tabitha was overdramatising the situation.

Jacob sat bolt upright. 'Yeah … she has a point. If we don't know why someone wanted to do away with the old bat, it could be some sort of sicko who's got our number next.'

I felt terrible that my thoughts had turned from Babcia to myself also, to Margot, to Remy. How could we know that we were safe until we knew what was going on? Was this a vendetta against Babcia, or was it something that involved all of us? None of it made sense. Unlike Tabitha and Jacob who had no shame in admitting their concern for themselves, I remained quiet on this point. It felt extremely poor form to be worrying about myself, while Babcia lay up the pathway dead. But, my body, my stupid body; it had a mind of its own. This realisation, this joining of these dots, caused another wave of panic through my body. My heart betrayed me again; it beat through my chest. *Steady, steady,* I said to myself.

'Surely, we can go home, and you can stay here and sort this all out?' Remy said quietly. I hadn't thought of Remy. Poor Remy. I had been so consumed by my own stupid panic. I couldn't see his face. He had turned his back to the group, looking away into the distance. His voice just trailed off.

'I'm sorry, Remy, really I am, but we all need to stay here until everyone is interviewed. Hopefully it won't be too long,' I heard William's voice crack a little here. I don't think he believed his own hopeful reassurance. I felt for William, standing here as human as the rest of us but needing to take charge, to herd a reluctant group who just want to disband, to get away from this scene.

'That's ridiculous,' someone said. I was surprised to realise it was Niles. His charm mask would surely completely come off now. I gripped Margot closer. We sank into our seats further, each in our own thoughts.

Finally, I could speak. Softly, I said, 'I can't … I can't believe it … I can't believe Babcia is in there at our party … alone … dead.'

I looked back up toward the arbour. At the other end, she lay motionless.

I tagged along as Margot and William walked to the far end of the leafy meeting place where they could keep an eye on the others but speak frankly out of earshot. As Margot led me by my hand, William started to protest but then gave up almost immediately. Margot had promised I'd stay by her side, and she meant it.

The two old friends shared a bit of a pathetic smile. They were clearly guarded about showing the personal side of their relationship to the group. William had abruptly changed roles and Margot, too, had adopted a business-like air.

Eventually, they spoke.

'You have to leave this for when the team arrives,' William said with firmness to Margot. His tone surprised me.

'Absolutely,' replied a strangely demure Margot.

'You mustn't interfere'. William now sounded as if he was almost begging.

'Of course,' said Margot.

William raised his eyebrows at Margot. 'You,' he emphasised 'mustn't interfere.'

'It's not my place,' confirmed Margot.

They stood together in silence. There was tension in this silence now.

'Okay.' He let out a deep sigh. 'What are you thinking? I know you, Margot; out with it.'

Margot just looked at him.

'Please don't play with me.' William looked stressed. I couldn't imagine having to step up and be responsible for this mess, not after what we all witnessed in the Birch Circle.

'I'm not playing with you.' Margot began to reach out to touch him, but she pulled herself back. Together they glanced at the many eyes watching them. I shuddered as I looked at them also. They were like nocturnal creatures glancing out from their prison. Eyes in the semi-darkness. While they were monitoring William, I'm sure they had little regard for Margot.

'This will be strange,' Margot finally said quietly.

'Will be? Don't you mean is strange?' William seemed to hang on Margot's every word. 'And do you really think it was murder? Could it have been a stroke or heart attack, or even choking? I mean, she wasn't young.'

'Weren't you there, William?' Margot's voice was sad but direct. 'She drank the vodka, and there was clearly poison in it that immediately killed her … gruesome.'

I shuddered again hearing this. I don't know why; my mind was circling around this image anyway.

'Yes, it was.' William hung his head.

Margot said quietly, 'Babcia wasn't choking, William. She wasn't gasping for air. She was being attacked from the inside. Can you go and have a look at her vodka glass please? You don't need to touch it, just smell it. See if there's any odour.'

The lights and sirens had arrived at this point. The crescendo of them coming closer and closer stopped abruptly on their arrival. I could never tell which siren means which emergency service … police, ambulance … I could never tell. William made noises about meeting them at the car park. 'I just need to go brief them.'

'Of course.'

'These will be general duties. As for the CIT … who knows. They're juggling a bit tonight. I just talked to Rob. He couldn't tell me when he'd get here … not immediately.'

'CIT?' I asked.

'Crime Investigation Team.'

'But you're heading up the investigation, aren't you, William?' Margot asked.

'Yes, I am.'

'And with you here … They won't exactly be in a rush?' Margot asked.

'Well … perhaps. The crew is pretty stretched tonight.' William seemed more sheepish than I'd seen him.

With this, William nodded his head. He was about to leave when a thought drew him back. 'Dean and Tabitha were right, I think. Until we understand this, we don't know if there is a further threat here tonight. We don't know if anyone else here might be in their line of sight … in danger.'

'Yes,' said Margot, 'until we can understand why someone wanted to kill Babcia, I think we could all be in danger … Not you, William. You're not actually part of this Narcissus Gardening Club circus. You're in the audience tonight.'

With a solemn nod of agreement, he turned on his heel and was gone. He waved his hands to the group commanding *stay,* as he passed by them. With both hands, he seemed to motion pushing back a tide. A bit like telling a pack of dogs to sit.

William's exit seemed to be an opening for Niles. Niles walked over to us. His shoulders rolled back. 'Anna, I need a word with you.'

I squeezed Margot's hand behind my back.

'No, not right now, Niles,' I managed to say.

'Stop being silly. Excuse me, Margot, but Anna and I need to talk.'

I knew Margot would intervene, but she held back to give me a chance to speak myself. 'Niles, it's not a good time.'

'Really! You're going to be like that! I thought we were adults here; don't make a scene.' He was warning me, *don't you dare.*

'Niles, I'm staying here.' My hand was clammy in Margot's.

Then Margot did step in. 'Niles, Anna has a choice. You need to respect her choice. It's not a good time.'

He shook his head and with a condescending smile

to Margot said, 'Margot, you don't understand. Anna and I are family. When times are difficult, family come together. She only has me … so if you don't mind … Anna and I are just going to take some time together. We have things to discuss.' I felt immediate nausea as I heard Niles' words. He would take threads of reality and weave them into some contorted version to try to pressure me, confuse me, manipulate me. But with Margot's strength by my side, I felt safer.

'Niles, how many times have I told you that I want to separate?'

'Anna, now's not the time, you get carried away sometimes. Besides, we can't let your anxiety have a voice here, or … you know … in our relationship.'

I had had enough. 'Margot is right, Niles. I have a choice. You need to listen to me. I don't want to speak to you, I don't want to be with you, I need you to go away.'

With this, Margot moved to stand in front of me. I would not have wanted to receive the expression that Margot then gave to Niles: it was firm; it was absolute. With this, Niles scoffed and walked back to the group. I watched him. He managed to return to the group with a lightness in his step, animated hands gesturing that he was dismissing us. He couldn't have the group know that he'd been rejected. An actor to the end.

I was glad to have a moment alone with Margot.

'Well done, you! Are you okay?' she asked as we

stood shoulder to shoulder looking out over the garden beds. You couldn't make out the plants like you could in daytime. They all looked like strange, dark figures standing to attention, some short, some tall, some thin, some bulbous and some with heads. They could look like different shaped goblins to a creative eye. In the distance you could see the silhouette of various trees. Most of the trees were evergreen, but some were deciduous. They had come out of their winter bones into the summer frocks.

Margot was staying true to her word; she kept me glued to her, or her to me. I held her hand or stood with her arm around me. Earlier, I had leaned into her shoulder from behind, our hands lightly touching. I kept my eye on Niles though. He saw my glare and looked at me with frustration, confusion … sometimes perhaps exasperation. I didn't care. I just found myself obsessively needing to keep an eye on him.

'Are you okay?' Margot said again.

'Yes,' I said.

'No, you're not,' Margot said gently.

'No, I'm not,' I agreed.

'But you will be; we'll get through this night.'

'Yes,' I said. 'I'm breathing now, not blacking out, so that's a good thing.'

I enjoyed the near silence as we stood there. I didn't know where I thought Niles would go as I kept glancing his way. I just needed to place him.

William rushed back through the arbour. He had been walking with a couple of police officers who then turned and went back up to the crime scene.

'General duties crew,' Margot said. 'They'll secure the crime scene, I expect.'

I was glad that I saw nothing of the ambulance attending to Babcia and taking her body away. The circus of emergency lights that came and went over the height of the trees was all we saw. William looked so drained; he was pale. He'd just walked from the macabre scene of Babcia lying there in the centre of the Birch Circle. I couldn't have done it.

He took a moment to catch his breath. He seemed to start mid-sentence. 'Her glass, her cup rather ... had been thrown on the ground. It was clearly hers as everyone else had theirs on the table area near where they'd stood,' he said.

Margot groaned.

'But don't worry,' William continued. 'It fell onto a crack and rested on the chair leg. It still had clear traces of a substance in it.'

'We have some good luck then ...' Margot said.

William sighed.

'And?'

'It had a distinct odour. I can't place it. I'm no expert on poisons, but there was a distinct odour that isn't the smell of vodka.'

'Yes, and vodka is odourless, or so they say ... At a

minimum, it doesn't have a distinct odour. Well done, our first piece of evidence.'

'Yes, it's something,' William agreed.

'Let's keep that up our sleeve.'

'Margot, we don't usually share evidence we find on the crime scene with civilians.'

'Yes, of course.' Margot strangely grinned.

'So?' William looked to Margot expectedly.

'Yes', Margot replied. 'You go. What's your summary?'

'Well …' he began, 'we have the when, we have the where and we presumably know the how. But the motive?'

'Exactly. It seems there's much more intrigue in the motive, the why, than the logistics of the murder.'

'Usually the how, when and the where leads to the guilty party,' William said.

'Exactly,' Margot agreed. 'Perhaps this is the hardest type of murder to solve. We were all there; we all could've done it. We all had opportunity. How many times did we all walk past her glass filled with vodka tonight? Many, many times.'

'All of us,' I heard myself say.

'Exactly.' Margot squeezed my shoulder. 'All of us.'

'True,' William wholeheartedly agreed.

Margot was concentrating. 'The murderer would be a fool if the purchase of the poison could be traced back to them, and of course they would have made sure there were no fingerprints. I doubt they're a fool. This was orchestrated. And the murderer would've had plenty of time to throw away the poison applicator and bottle throughout the garden, with no prints when we find it. Let's see, but I doubt it'll be useful.'

'Yes,' agreed William. 'This was clever and calculated. We'll start looking for the container when my crime scene crew arrive.'

'At least you'll be able to confirm the poison … but without fingerprints …'

'We might be able to source where the poison was purchased.'

'Maybe … but I doubt that we'll find anything useful … Worth checking, of course.'

Margot and William were painting a very bleak picture. William looked increasingly morose as they brainstormed. He was becoming agitated. Signs of sweat snuck through his cotton shirt. I could see his chest rise and fall. I think William was starting to go down my path, my hideous experience of panic. He looked so calm and in command to begin with, but here he was falling apart before my eyes. In contrast, Margot seemed to be becoming more composed and collected, resolute even.

'So, poison,' William said, as if to himself.

'A particularly vicious poison,' Margot added. 'They certainly did their research and found something immediately deadly. They made sure there was no way that she could survive … that we as a group … immediately on the scene couldn't revive her. Truly ruthless.'

We stood in contemplation. I'd resolved to remain completely silent. This wasn't my conversation. Margot and William were engrossed in the meeting of their minds. It seemed like they had forgotten that I was there, and I was perfectly fine with that.

Margot continued, 'Poor Babcia. I had such a soft spot for her. Whoever did this has to be found.'

'Absolutely.' William leaned toward Margot and lowered his head. 'I've never seen anything like it. I usually turn up after they're deceased. This was just horrible. Beyond horrible.'

'Yes, just horrible, beyond words.' Margot had joined him as she lost herself in thought. 'All we have to tunnel toward is motive,' she murmured. 'You wouldn't happen to have a list of the names of everyone here, would you?'

'Actually, I do. Babcia's personal assistant, Ms Idoia, was a gem. Babcia told her to help me with anything I needed: the running of this place, her personal history, her finances, everything. Babcia was surprisingly open. Turns out that Idoia actually ran or chaired this community garden, not Babcia. Babcia was just involved for her pleasure. Which is fair enough.'

My head spun. So William's investigation involved Babcia and not to any small degree given he'd burrowed into her personal world, her personal information, like that. Surely, whatever he was up to circled around Babcia. I was lost. I had no idea what was going on.

'The list then?' Margot said.

William pulled out a small, well-used notebook from his pocket, and in a moment was able to present the list to Margot. William stole a glance at the group hunched on their chairs. Their eyes watched his every movement. All of them, I noticed, except Remy. Remy just kept gazing into the distance.

In scrawled writing the list read:

Narcissus Gardening Club Committee Members:

Anna Humphrey

Jacob Clarin

Margot Gray

Dean Papoutsis

Tabitha Luhmann

Frowning, Margot glared at the list and then nodded her head.

'Remy's not on there?'

'No,' said William. He seemed to only be noticing this now.

Margot stared off into the distance. 'Give me a minute, William.' She turned slightly. She was quiet, eerily quiet. Every now and then she shook her head from side to side. I'd have just loved to visit her thoughts as they cycled. She then extended herself for a brief walk, while I was content to stay with William. Only a matter of metres away, she returned her loop to where we stood. She reached for me again; this had become our way.

She slowly looked up at William. He had such a keen expression on his face as he glanced off into the distance. Her next words were slow and delicate, 'So do you want to solve this murder, William?'

He slowly turned and lowered his eyes to meet hers.

She continued, 'What if there is more than one person here with a motive? What if this murder isn't solved by the police? What if by not solving it, there is a second murder? If someone murders once for a motive, perhaps it's even easier to murder a second time for the same motive.'

William turned his back to the group, fear rippling across his face. Fear and confusion. At no point did he dismiss what to me seemed like Margot making an exaggerated statement. No, he was sombre; he was taking her words seriously. I was sure William was torn. I took him to be a man of policies and procedures, and here he was talking with Margot, the lateral-thinking wildcard.

'What are you saying?'

'We need to know who and why, and we have precious little time to establish this. We have a pressure cooker here, ready to explode. If we stir it a bit, the truth may come out … We need this pressure to combust. What's the harm in trying?'

'Margot, Margot, I know you; you're like a dog with a bone. You won't want to leave this be, to the police process, but you must.'

William was again pleading. He was pleading for restraint, but like me, I'm sure he was curious to know Margot's line of thought. The poor man's stress was growing. Perhaps one path was procedure, but the other path involved Margot's insights, insights that he would have craved to know. Insights that might lead to a stealthy conclusion.

William seemed to crumble into resignation when Margot went on to say, 'I have threads to pull. I have a picture forming.'

'What! Proof? Evidence of something?'

'I'm afraid not, but threads for sure. If we pull at the threads, let's see. Let's see if they unravel.'

'Margot, what are you actually talking about?'

'Let me think. Let's start with what you've got. What's your brief?'

'Fair enough … Babcia came to our attention about three weeks ago. She had received anonymous threats in her letterbox and bricks thrown onto her property.'

I was startled to hear this, but Margot just listened intently.

'Babcia contacted the police over that? That doesn't sound like her,' Margot said.

'No, you're right. Remy contacted the police.'

'Oh, that makes sense.'

'And we were trying to establish any connections, any links with Babcia, people she might know, but she lived an extremely insular life. Just Babcia, Remy and some friendly neighbours.'

'Neighbours?'

'Yes, apparently Babcia was the heart of her neighbourhood, always helping people out, looking out for them, sharing her produce.'

'Well, who knew! That could come from her growing up in a small community'?

'Perhaps … so apart from her neighbourhood, Remy and her PA, Ms Idoia was what she called her, the only contact that Babcia had with the outside world was the Narcissus Gardening Club. So that's why we organised for me to come along … you know … to have a look around.'

'And you saw my name on the list and you didn't tell me?' Margot frowned at him playfully.

'You can't have all the surprises.'

Margot sneaked him a wink.

I turned away to hide my face. They couldn't see that I was waiting for them to mention Niles' name sooner or later. I listened. Every word seemed to stretch out as I waited for his name.

William had hesitated. 'Margot really …' I knew that he was looking at me. Signalling to me with his eyes. Signalling for me to go.

'William, this is our position tonight. It's not going to change. We are juggling two crises here.'

'Yes – but, Margot, this is a police investigation now. You work with the police. But respectfully, Anna …' I could feel his eyes on me, but I wasn't going to budge. Despite William's logic, Margot somehow stood resolute.

There seemed to be a stand-off between them. Rubbing his brow and letting out a deep sigh, William continued, 'We need to question someone with regard to these intimidating actions toward Babcia …' He hesitated again. 'Niles.'

Niles!

'Wait!' I said. 'But he doesn't – she didn't – they don't *know* each other …'

William said gently, 'I'm sorry, Anna.'

My head was spinning. 'Are you saying they *did* know each other?'

'I'm afraid I'll have to ask you some questions' – he glanced at Margot – 'when you're ready, of course.'

'I'm not with Niles anymore,' I blurted.

Margot spun around to face me. She cupped my face in her hands and kissed my forehead. A sad yet joyful smile on her face. From my peripheral vision I saw movement within the group. They had been trying to decode our charades I'm sure, and now we were just confusing them more.

'What's going on?' Jacob shouted over to us. His voice

seemed to shatter the silence that had hung around us.

William was brilliant. He brought his hand up, palm to Jacob and motioned downward. It was amazing to see William behaving with such power. But it worked. Jacob was silent.

I searched for William's next words. Surely he would elaborate on how on earth Niles was mixed up with Babcia. My mind was spinning. William's words *We need to question someone with regard to these intimidating actions toward Babcia* were whirring in my head like a ball ricocheting around inside a tin barrel. When you feel like you're avalanching off a mountain, there's a point where added momentum or extra mud really doesn't make that much difference. That is how I felt. While my mind was racing, I strangely just felt numb, for the moment anyway.

With this, William asked with an apologetic smile, 'I understand the state that you're in Anna, or at least I think I do,' he said, 'and I wouldn't ask this of you unless it was crucial. But I truly need a moment alone with Margot.'

I looked to Margot.

'Your decision,' she gently said.

With this, I took several steps away from them. It was never a question of walking toward the group, toward Niles. I walked in the opposite direction. I preferred the darkness. Standing in that black garden, alone, with only flickers of light, I couldn't help but hear a few words from the conversation that was supposed to be kept private from me.

It was Margot's voice I could hear. She clearly couldn't suppress the astonishment in her voice. 'That's extraordinary … Does she know? Well that puts a completely different spin on everything … She's linked now … William, you have this all wrong.'

My eavesdropping had not helped my cause. I tried to imagine even more torturous versions of what kind of mess Niles had got me into. I wanted to stop hearing them, but I couldn't. Every word, every syllable, led me to confusion, to fear. Somehow Niles had not only buried himself in some crisis, but me as well.

*

I had come up with no ideas that made sense as I rejoined them minutes later. For Niles to want to intimidate Babcia, he would have had to know her. But he didn't … or did he? If Niles had done something corrupt, something I could imagine him being arrogant enough to try to do, then again, why would this involve Babcia? And fraud wouldn't involve intimidation of a random old lady who he doesn't know. No matter how I turned this over in my mind, I couldn't make sense of any of it. I braced myself for what was to come.

'My beautiful, William.' Margot was looking out at the silhouette of trees in the darkness. She spoke as if lost in thought. 'It's pure tragedy, pure tragedy what has happened here tonight … pure tragedy. I feel sick. That will stay with us forever … that image of her. I feel so utterly devastated for Babcia. That was so cruel. So ruthless. My heart breaks … but …'

'But?'

'Actually, there is no "but".'

'I know you, Margot,' William said. 'There is a "but"!'

With open palms extended toward us, Margot said with earnest. 'We must focus on finding her answers no matter what. We must have justice for Babcia. Babcia deserves justice and would want justice.'

William nodded with a solemn frown.

'Life is a strange game; we're all just small, ridiculous pieces on the board. I think tonight we'll discover just how ridiculous we humans can be. We have a motley crew here. By destabilising one domino piece, I sense they will all come down. Now is the time to roll up our sleeves and delicately peel back the layers.'

'Margot, be kind to them!'

'What are you talking about.' I raised my eyes to meet theirs, flicking between Margot and William, trying to understand.

'Anna, beautiful … William is heading up this investigation and he has two choices. He can either wait for the rest of the crew to arrive before interviewing the witnesses, or he can get started now.'

'Okay?' I said. I felt my crossed arms cradle me as I held myself tight.

'… And William has decided.'

'Don't you mean … been convinced!'

She ignored him. 'William has decided that we can make a go of it now, make a start. I have worked extensively with the police consulting them with complex cases, so I may as well help out now.'

'Help out …' William chuckled. 'Don't you mean take the lead and keep me in the dark. Margot, as I said, be kind.'

'Some deserve kindness, some do not,' she replied firmly.

'I swear, Margot, you were put on this earth to make me feel uncomfortable.'

As they turned to walk back toward the group, Margot leaned over to William and quietly whispered, 'This picture reminds me of a field of wilting sunflowers.'

'I'm lost,' whispered William as we approached.

'Have you ever seen it? A depressing field of wilting sunflower plants. Their decaying black flower heads cowering at your glance.'

CHAPTER VII

The initial shock had moved to a solemn, macabre feeling amongst us. The darkness of the surrounding gardens was mirrored by the darkness within the group.

Shattering this silence, Tabitha let out a howl, 'Oh, this is too much. What horror! I admired her so much. We were just getting close.' She cradled her face in her hands. 'I don't know how I'll cope with this. It's too much, too much … more than I can bear.'

This performance seemed to wake Remy up. 'Sorry?' he thundered, all politeness gone.

Tabitha, lost in her hysteria, continued, 'We must remember. We must take some time to cherish her, our beloved Babcia.'

'You didn't even like her, Tabitha. You detested her,' Margot said now standing in front of the group. The full presence of Margot was about to be felt.

'Yeah, you had nothing but contempt for her,' I burst forward. I shared in Remy and Margot's disgust. How could she be so fake and attention-seeking during this genuine tragedy? It was just sickening. 'This isn't about you, Tabitha. Can you tolerate not being relevant?'

I received grins of appreciation from Remy and Jacob. This was hardly a brave move from me as I stood slightly behind Margot, plugged to her like an anxious child.

Tabitha went from tears to a stone-cold voice. It was like flicking a switch; the contrast was chilling. 'Well, did you like her Anna? Who here actually liked Babcia? Who will actually feel her loss?'

Remy stood up; he held his body to attention and then dropped his head in respect.

William looked at him with admiration. 'Yes Remy, you had a genuine care for her'.

Margot added, 'Actually I'd say that I enjoyed her character very, very much. I had a deep fondness for her. And there were many people who actually benefited from Babcia.'

'I feel sick', I said, suddenly aware of this pain in my stomach. I didn't quite need to vomit but it was sitting there, bubbling away.

Jacob jumped in, 'Yeah, there's all this food here, but I'm sure no one will be eating for a long time.'

'I'm going to miss her Babciaisms,' I said quietly to myself as much as to the group.

'Sorry, her what'? asked William.

Remy interjected, 'Her Babcia talk, her sayings. I didn't know what she was talking about half the time. I'd just kind of guess at what she meant.'

'Babcia was all about sharing her important life lessons whether you wanted to hear them or not,' Margot said. 'Pessimism, sharp objects, animals and wagons: they seem to be the themes of her Polish words of wisdom. Using such colourful language, Babcia just kept pulling them out. She sure kept me on my toes. She was an absolute treasure trove of bizarre, dark and, I think often, hilarious language.' Margot was sadly smiling as she shook her head slowly.

'Bizarre, for sure,' Jacob said, as he played with his wedding ring, his usual, absent-minded habit.

'Babcia knew more ways to call you an idiot than anyone,' Margot concluded. She spoke with such affection.

I liked that we were taking a moment to talk about Babcia. I felt a level of respect in this.

Niles was edgy. He eyeballed William. 'So, you're with the police?'

'Yes,' William said simply.

'And what are you doing here?' Niles firmly enquired.

'Well, let me explain.' William looked to Margot, who in turn gave him a confirming nod. 'I'm here having only started preliminary work on a case, this case.'

'Case?' said Tabitha.

'Babcia had been receiving death threats for a few weeks now, and due to her excessive wealth and vulnerable age, we've taken it very seriously.'

'We?' said Dean.

'The police,' William clarified.

'Wealthy?'

'Yes, very, very wealthy. Babcia is …' William corrected himself, 'Babcia *was* the creator and owner of the largest storage-unit business on the east coast. Our grounded Babcia was a multi-millionaire many times over.'

'That bitch!' Dean abruptly stood up and started pacing.

I shuddered.

'I suggest you calm yourself and sit down.' William walked toward him as if herding him to a seat.

Dean took his seat with an angry shake of his head.

'It can't be possible,' Niles said. I could see the muscles in his jaw clenching. He had a snarling, carnivore quality to him.

'How can you resent someone who is self-made? When it's completely through their determination and hard work?' Margot said. 'Babcia was a smart business-woman … super smart, strategic and determined. She and her husband got in early to the storage market … before there was a storage market in fact.'

Storage? *How peculiar; that's* our *business area. How bizarre.* My mind whirled again. Perhaps this had some-thing to do with business competition? I don't see how though. Niles would be small fish compared to what I was hearing of Babcia.

Margot wasn't finished. 'And they came to dominate

a huge chunk of the market. Just as the western world started buying more than they could fit into their homes, the storage unit became essential. Another cost of living it seemed. Nowak Storage, you would have heard of it.'

From Dean's startled expression, he clearly recognised this name. Tabitha and Jacob, however, didn't seem to react. As for Niles, for the first time tonight, he averted his eyes and his face from the group. This was the only time tonight that I did want to see him. I wanted to see his reaction.

'They say her business holds a monopoly …' Margot continued. 'It's close.' Margot looked like she was enjoying sharing Babcia's achievements. I liked that Margot was taking pleasure in championing Babcia in her absence. Tears welled up in me.

'Well, clearly it was Remy!' launched a frothing Dean. 'He was the only person likely to benefit from her death. She liked him, and she liked *no one,*' he almost yelled. 'Remy has been here working his way in, worming his way to her money. She was besotted by him. He made her blind. He fixed … he fixed it so that when she died, he's right there ready to snatch her money. Look at her will; my bet is you'll find she left it all to *him.*'

Remy laughed sadly. He brought his head to his hands in dismay.

'You laugh but you were in finance before you had your bullshit sea change, right?' Dean spat. 'You pretended to be her gardener, but I'm willing to bet you were actually managing her money. Maybe you weren't even waiting for her to die; maybe you've already been putting some aside for yourself. You were embezzling from her! And now with her dying, she'll never find out.' Dean looked so proud of himself with these wild allegations.

'Man, you're daft,' Remy said. 'I'm the one who contacted the police! I was trying to convince Babcia to get private security, but she wouldn't. She was as stubborn as ever. She never spent her money. She lived as she grew up, a total spendthrift to the end. I've been so … so stressed about this very thing happening. All my fears here have come true. And you accuse me?'

Remy put his head back into his hands and curled over into himself. 'I failed. It happened right in front of me, and I didn't see anything. I failed her.'

William was quick to quash this line of talk. 'Remy, you miss that we were all there, none of us saw it.' William seemed caught up himself here. 'I'm a police officer, and I was actually on duty. It was right under my nose as well. This murder happened in front of all of us, Remy. Don't blame yourself. It wasn't your fault. There was *nothing* you could have done.'

'Yeah, Detective Tarlington,' Tabitha snarled aggressively. 'You're the one who failed here.' There was a sound of shocked gasps. 'You were actually employed to protect her right? That was your job and *you* failed.'

'Tabitha'! Remy stood up and stormed toward her.

'It's okay.' William stepped in. He gestured for Remy to move away.

It seemed to me that William was his firmest and strongest when action was required of him. You wouldn't know that he was the same person who had earlier stood with Margot and me at a distance, clearly experiencing waves of anxiety. He didn't even bother to answer Tabitha's comment.

'You're all fools,' Tabitha's voice shrilled again. 'It was Anna! Didn't you see when Babcia was dying? Who'd she search for … look for? Who'd she stare at? It was creepy. When she was gasping for dear life, she eyeballed Anna. It was blood-curdling. Babcia stared down Anna as she took her last gasp. Why else would she search for her? Anna is the murderer!'

'That's enough,' William snapped at her again. 'Babcia didn't know what was going on. The poor thing was in a state of mortal terror.'

'Pft!' Tabitha raised her hand at William as if she could block his words.

I didn't take to heart what Tabitha was saying; it merely brought me back to my own thoughts. Babcia had searched for me. She'd locked her eyes on me, and then remained frozen there. Why? I had already been tortured by this question. Why? She died staring into me while her eyes showed me the terror and the excruciating pain of her death. Her moment of death was extremely personal to me because she drew me into it. I wished she hadn't. With immense feeling, I wished she hadn't. This just added to the layers of images flashing constantly before my eyes.

'How sure are you that it was murder?' asked Remy, his tone desperate.

William quietly replied, 'Well, at this stage, there's reason to suspect that it was poison from her vodka shot. Something pretty potent to kill her so quickly and violently.' With a heavy tone, he said, 'And if this is the case, then any one of us could've done it. We all walked past her filled glass numerous times. Anyone could've dropped the poison in from the time it was poured to when she drank her fatal shot.' William looked at Margot, and with this statement he triggered Margot's dominos to cascade. I took this as a gesture of commitment from him to Margot that the show was hers. The group had no clue that he'd passed the baton and that they were about to experience Margot at full throttle.

Tabitha piped up, 'Maybe someone else, an outsider, did it; a felon?'

'Yes,' replied William turning to her, 'if it was murder, a felon did do it, but it almost definitely has to be a felon right here amongst us.' There was a shudder across the group as William said this. 'It can only be one of us who had access to Babcia's vodka glass that sat there in plain sight. No stranger entered our little party, and there was always someone in the Birch Circle. Several people usually. The evidence indicates that there is a cold-hearted killer amongst us. Someone here had a major grudge against Babcia. Someone wanted Babcia dead, and they achieved it!'

With me as her shadow, Margot walked slowly, step by step to stand next to William. She took her time, saying, 'I don't agree with you there, Detective Sergeant Tarlington'. She was reminding them of his rank. Clever, I thought. 'You think there is one dark individual here who had a motive to kill Babcia? I'd argue that there are many.'

Eyes turned as if in slow motion toward Margot. She had been largely irrelevant in the shadow of William and now she came forward to presume centre stage.

'Are you all innocent?' she said.

Everyone's night eyes flashed with alarm at Margot. She looked around this outdoor space, scattered trees moving gently in the wind, the floor lined by sifting dry leaves. Our seating area was punctuated with aging timber sheds, a place for garden equipment, and para-phernalia. There was a slight ramshackle quality to the space. Pots, wound hoses and tools lay around. While they had not been put away, they were neatly placed. Rambling garden paths headed off in various direc-tions. A beautiful setting for a harrowing evening.

Margot continued without needing encouragement or invitation, 'Tonight, as we map out events, it may look like a case of coincidence and omens. But we'll discover that everything was, in truth, planned, and consequences have directly come to many.' Margot sounded almost prophetic. She spoke firmly but with an understated calmness. 'I think you're a circus of flawed and vulnerable characters each trying to withstand and survive the storm that you've created for yourselves.' Margot was starting to speak in Babcia riddles.

In unison, many protests could be heard.

'Whoa up, that's a bit harsh,' Dean barked, gripping the table in front of him. He spread his fingers out with a clawing effect.

'Excuse me?' hissed Tabitha.

'This will be good,' Remy said, his tone was grim.

'You have some nerve,' bellowed Jacob.

William stood statue-like, arms crossed. A vein was pulsing in his neck.

'That's harsh, is it?' Margot stood with authority, and then with a slow intentional walk approached Dean, her head lowered, her eyes looking along the length of her nose as if peering over invisible glasses.

Dean scoffed, 'What are you about? You're no official. You need to keep out of this.'

Margot then began to gently pace. I stepped backwards. I was happy to momentarily unlock from her, provided that she stood between me and the group, or more to the point, between Niles and me. Margot was taking the stage, and I didn't want to join her.

On cue, William stepped slightly forward, drawing

the group's attention. 'Actually, this *is* Margot's official occupation. As a clinical psychologist, she also consults for the police force on complex forensic cases. It is a coup for the station that she happens to be here on hand tonight.'

He turned again to the group. 'Margot is an expert on these dark matters, with an absolute wealth of experience … on the matters of the criminal mind. Margot is a bit of an icon in our small law-enforcement pocket of the world. Everyone knows about Dr Margot Gray.'

Jacob screwed his face up in contempt and said, 'But … but she has aqua glitter nail polish on! Do you expect me to listen to someone with aqua glitter nail polish?'

'I don't care what you think, quite frankly,' was William's response.

We were learning quickly that this wasn't the reserved man who we had first met earlier in the evening. We were learning about his capacity to take command. I imagined that with a situation as precarious as this, he was hoping that everyone would stay in line. I sensed that a lot of this was an act for him. He was masking from the group the subtle clues of anxiety that I had been privy to, working to maintain his professional face. Despite his display, I could see his hands shaking. It was slight, he hide them behind his back. They were to never see this side of him.

I was intrigued by how the group would respond to

Margot. I imagined they would struggle. They had so much history with Margot being here while in social mode. I was sure Margot's carefree way would lead people to underestimate her exceptional substance.

Margot ignored this distraction. She spoke quietly, with a low voice that commanded attention. She clearly wouldn't be looking for anyone's approval. 'Well, the first clue was pretty simple.'

In unison, everyone hushed.

'There's more than one of you who doesn't actually like gardening!' said Margot.

Remy laughed, a release of nervous tension.

Margot continued, 'So, the question beckons, why are you here?' Her voice was firm but with no form of aggression.

'Is that it?' Tabitha scoffed.

Margot ignored her entirely.

'The devil is in the detail with you lot … but may I say that William … and Remy in fact,' Margot nodded to him, 'bring additional information that you, and until moments ago, I was not privy to.' There was silence. 'There are three pieces of information that Babcia shared with the police … the threats to her, a business dealing and a relationship. None of these pieces of information explain our situation neatly, but they *do* assist us.'

Margot took a moment; she looked into everyone's eyes, one at a time, unapologetic. 'We're going to look at each of you.' Not only did she have a time limit before the police cavalry arrived, but she clearly had a strategy. I was intrigued to see how this would play out … how the situation would unravel.

Margot was clearly not going to hold back. 'Remy has been accused of stealing from Babcia, or perhaps at a minimum, getting into her good favour so that upon her death, he'll benefit.'

'Remy? You're questioning Remy?' I was startled by how high pitched my words sounded as they came out of my mouth. I trusted Margot implicitly, but I just couldn't handle the thought of Remy being brought into question; you don't attack behind allied lines.

Niles shot me a look of fury. He then turned to study Remy's response. I was sure that he thought he'd catch a moment between us. He was fuming. No doubt he was fantasising about how he'd *sort this out* with me when we got home. How he would *sort me* out. But I was never going home with him again. Tonight had brought me crashing to earth, no more treading water, not for an instant. Relief came from this clarity. One positive from tonight.

Niles suddenly stood up, thrusting his chair backwards. 'Would you stop defending Fetch. Your crush on him makes you a blind idiot!'

I shuddered and stepped back into the edge of a garden bed. I almost lost my balance on the uneven brick work. I gathered myself, stood tall and worked to hold his intense eye contact. He'd have seen my quiver; he knew the tell of my lips.

'Who?' Dean asked, glancing around with interest.

'She has names for all of you,' Niles said, pointing his finger at me and then waving it between the members. I braced myself. I begged him silently to stop. 'Didn't you know?' He continued, 'Queen Babcia, Tabitha is Princess.' He gestured a mocking bow to Tabitha. Tabitha was startled, but then seemed pleased. 'Dean the … the General. And you Jacob … Jacob the Jester. Nice, hey!' He scoffed. Niles was on full reveal of his nasty side now. His paranoid jealousy had him come undone.

'But what did you just say? Fetch?' Dean said.

'Yeah, fucking Fetch over there.'

He was trying to humiliate me, and it was working. My head hung low, I didn't care about any of them, but the thought of offending Remy mortified me. I just wanted to crawl into the ground.

'That's brilliant.' These words from Remy came as a shock to me. I looked up to see him grinning broadly at me, his eyes seemed to smile at me. 'I really needed a laugh. Brilliant, Anna.'

I smiled an apology to him. He just winked.

'What about Margot?' asked Tabitha; she clearly wasn't offended. I imagined that she'd actually choose her name herself: Princess.

Niles didn't answer. This wasn't going the way he'd

wanted it. No one seemed offended. I daresay most were hearing a compliment.

I looked at Margot sheepishly.

'Go on,' Tabitha demanded.

'Goddess,' I said quietly, wanting this moment to be over.

Tabitha scoffed loudly. Margot's name had trumped hers. Margot just grinned.

'Brilliant!' Remy said again.

Margot then snapped straight back into business mode. 'It's true that Babcia was fond of Remy, but … many of you may struggle with this concept … Babcia was fond of Remy because he treated Babcia well.'

Jacob laughed angrily.

'Yes,' continued Margot. 'He earned her positive opinion. He'd proven himself trustworthy which is no small thing for Babcia. Babcia, I thought, trusted no one until I saw that she trusted Remy. And she trusted him why? Because he is trustworthy; it's that simple.'

'He was her accountant and then became her personal gardener? Come on!' Dean said, shaking his head, a sneer on his face.

In a calm, deep voice, Margot continued, 'Yes, Remy was originally Babcia's financial advisor. Babcia was right there by Remy's side when he decided to unsub-scribe from his high-paying, fast-paced world. Quite the opposite of the behaviour of someone who is money hungry, wouldn't you agree? Did they continue to talk about money and business efforts? Well, I hope so! Intelligent people do talk over things with those who have shared skill levels. He became her confidant and what a blessing for her as she needed one. Babcia was, after all, very alone in her world. That's why Remy often appeared to be the only person who she wasn't rude to.'

Despite the protests only a moment earlier, we settled again into a trance, listening closely to Margot's every word. There was almost a stupor of silence.

Then she said, 'Now, who shall we discuss next?' After scanning the peering faces, Margot looked up at William. I saw a moment of sparkle in her eyes. He seemed to brace himself. 'Actually, if you'll forgive me, I first need to confer with Detective Tarlington over an important detail. You'll of course notice that I'm keeping Anna with me, that's because we can't afford another body drop tonight. After a panic attack of Anna's magnitude, with tonight's crisis, there's a high chance that she'll have another one. So, I'm keeping her within arms' reach. So I apologise for her preferential treatment, but I'm multi-tasking here.'

With that she walked up to me and gently took my hand, and we three again walked back to our previous position in the garden. Sneaking a glance backward, I saw Dean, Jacob, Niles and Tabitha all craning their necks in our direction. Remy, however, had resumed his slumped position, staring off to who knows where.

Margot and I were touching with mere fingertips,

but that was enough for me.

With a heavy tone and eyes pleading for understanding, William said, 'What is it?'

Careful to also speak in a whisper, Margot replied, 'Nothing.'

'Nothing?' he said, animated in his surprise.

We were still in view of the others, I could see them watching us. I was sure that they would have read William's reaction as a response to Margot saying something of importance. I was irrelevant during all these proceedings, which was what I wanted.

Margot nodded. 'Yes, nothing!'

William – and I – waited for her to explain.

Finally, Margot obliged, 'But William, we must appear as if we're talking about a *something*. A very important something. A something that we must whisper with determined secrecy in a very serious tone between us.'

'If I'm to be part of your ploy, you sure as hell need to do better than that. Fill me in for goodness sake.'

Margot frowned at him. 'Of course.' The pressure between them was creating some crack lines. 'The crucial detail is that for this to work we must create a certain level of stress in our audience.'

'Stress! You want stress!' William said. 'I have an absolute elephant sitting on my chest … My heart is racing so hard I feel like I should go get it checked … and you say we need to *create* stress!'

'Yes,' said Margot, reaching for and squeezing his shoulder, 'but you're doing really well.'

I'd never have imagined when I was hyperventilating back at the Birch Circle, having my panic attack, that the person who perhaps could most relate to my anxious state was William. He had looked so calm and composed. I was sure this was why he was being so patient with me there, clinging on to Margot. I felt great respect for William as it was apparent that he routinely found the courage to out-manoeuvre his anxiety.

'Don't you think it's already been a sufficiently stressful night?' William returned to his earlier point. There was a tone of irritated sarcasm in his voice.

'Yes, of course,' said Margot, 'but I'm talking about their personal anxiety here. You see, my dear William, anxiety is anticipation of something … of fear, of the unknown; our thoughts fill in the blanks about what could happen. We need to let them torture themselves with their own imagination of what might happen next. They each have their secrets, so let them load their own gun, let their stress implode and expose them. Their minds can torture them plenty without us needing to do a thing. Time is our friend here, William. Anticipation. We shall stand here and speak of whispered nothings, while they sit there in excruciating contemplation of what is being said, of what might be exposed. Let them fear.'

'You're cruel,' William said.

'Yes,' agreed Margot.

'When you need to be,' I added.

'Thank you, Anna.'

'But Margot, we're on a timeline; we don't know how long we've got.'

'Yes,' I could hear a crackle of fear in her voice, 'but you said your crime investigation team was held up.'

'Well, yes, but—'

'And they're going to contact you with how things are progressing.'

'Yes.'

'Well, it looks like we've got a little time.'

'Yes … but.'

'Look don't get me wrong, this is a gamble. But we must do this right, William. If we rush it, if we don't follow my plan, then we'll botch it. Our opportunity to find Babcia's murderer will be lost. This is a very subtle and complex picture. I don't know if police processes will unlock this one. As you know the police system can be a crude machine when it's a delicate situation.'

I was astounded. I wanted the rest of the police to come quickly. I wanted to just get out of there, but Margot and William were focussed on actually prolonging the night, prolonging the torture. They seemed glad of time; they actually wanted the police to be delayed. Margot even seemed somehow to be beginning to enjoy this challenge.

'I must play this evening with great delicacy,' she

said. 'This could go either way, but if we play it right …'

'This doesn't feel right, Margot.'

'Trust me!' said Margot with a slice of humour.

'I don't have a choice it seems.' And with this William cracked a resigned smile back at her. 'So how do we do this?'

'Well, we're halfway there; we just keep talking.'

'Hang on …' And with this, William took out his phone. He swiftly rang and informed his colleague that this was not an urgent situation. Everything was settled here. We were prepared to wait.

Before he signed off, he casually mentioned '… and we have Margot Gray here. Yes, that's right; we expected her to be here … A member, yes … Yes, very handy … I will … I will … right … Let me know how things are progressing with you … Yes … Well that's all you can do.'

William's call was like a piece of theatre that was certainly not missed by the audience of eyes upon us.

'They're busy than?' Margot asked.

'Yes … Right … what are we doing? What are we talking about?'

'Say …' Margot looked up as if searching her mind, 'cooking?'

'Cooking?'

With care to converse in a serious whisper and serious tone, they began to chat. This was a pantomime for them to play out; I again had no part in it.

'Are you still accosting people with your cooking?' Margot said almost under her breath. 'You know, Anna, William really needs to stop cooking.'

'Bridie's been whinging to you, hasn't she? My beautiful wife just doesn't understand that I show my love through cooking.'

'But William, you're a terrible cook.'

'You know lately I've tried baking. I'm bad at baking,' William mused.

Margot groaned quietly. 'You don't say? How can someone be such a competent detective, so good at detail and following protocol and not be able to cook?'

'The girls won't even try my cooking anymore.'

'Smart girls.'

William whispered to me, 'My cooking never seems edible. I actually make people sick.'

As they rambled on about baking and the detective's deficiencies in the kitchen, my mind wandered. I knew Niles was an arsehole, but would he really murder someone? And what was his connection with Babcia? Margot was being protective of me tonight for sure. As much as I appreciated and needed this, I couldn't help but wonder if she had another agenda. Did she think that I was in danger based on this extra information that William had shared with her? *Surely, if there is information relating to me ... I have a right to know.* I had been contemplating this, wondering if I had the courage to broach this with them. The truth was, I felt so fragile that I didn't trust my own judgement. I decided not to make any waves and just see how this played out. Despite this resolution, or you could say, cop out, I felt resentment rising in me toward Margot and William. If it was something to do with me … then I should surely be the first to know. Not the last.

We stood together, working to look very solemn with our body language. Somehow, we had not been pestered. Both William and Margot turned to look at the group, and I followed suit. Five sets of eyes were gazing at us in anticipation.

Margot was momentarily quiet. Her mind was clearly on its next challenge. Her tone turned sombre. 'Shall we get this done? We're going to have to crack some eggs!' Her voice was firm and resolute. She turned on her heel, and we followed.

Margot and William walked slowly back to resume their positions at the front of the group. The members regathered, all but Dean who was on the phone at a slight distance behind one of the tool sheds. We affectionately called this timber shed the Tardis, its size and shape was so impractical. I had hung back, not in a hurry to return to The Hub gathering, so I was therefore in position to overhear his conversation at a stretch. Did I intentionally listen to him? I don't know. Nevertheless, these are the words I heard him say. 'It's all over now. You hear me. It's all over. You've got nothing!' He growled. He kept his voice down, but his seething anger was unmistakable.

I scurried back to Margot and William and took my place behind them. William stood with his arms behind his back, hands grasped together.

'Niles!' Margot bellowed out loud and stunned us all. Niles, as usual, expressed his stress with anger. His nostrils quivered as he worked to stare Margot down. Margot faced Niles with clear eyes and an expressionless face. She created a great sense of momentum as she spoke.

'Some people live their life in an echo chamber, Niles. They promenade a scripted version of themselves for the world. The way they want people to see them. But it's a façade; their life is actually hollow. You think your happiness equates to what you project to others.' Then Margot's tone change. She said flatly, 'Niles, why are you here?'

'Well to have time with my wife of course!'

I felt a hit in my gut. Hearing his words *my wife*. No longer. He was trying to sound firm and controlled. Surely he was waking up to the fact that he couldn't manipulate or intimidate Margot.

'Really, a couple who want to have time together don't usually go to committee social events. And Niles, were you invited? Or did you invite yourself? Did Anna even agree to you coming tonight? Or did you impose yourself on her? I'd even ask, how many times in the last six months have you prioritised time with Anna?'

Niles' eyes narrowed.

Margot didn't wait for these answers. Niles didn't provide them. 'But my question is why … Why are you here, Niles?'

Margot looked to William. He took the hint. 'Yes, this is the question I have been wanting answered tonight. In line with our investigation, it makes no sense that you are here tonight. The question is an important one. Why are you here tonight, Niles?'

There was continued silence from Niles. He ignored William and seemed determined to keep staring at Margot. The crimson colour rose in his face, a sweating complexion came over him.

In a very business-like tone Margot continued, 'Babcia kindly informed Detective Tarlington that she was actually your silent partner in your small storage company from the very beginning.'

These words threw me off balance. What was Margot talking about?

She continued, 'She was your source for extra funds, and of late you've even pressed her for extra money to save your business from going bust … despite her historically receiving no dividends on her investment. She had no face-to-face dealings with you, but of course, she studied your conduct from afar. And would you say … would you confidently say, William, that she didn't have a good opinion of Niles' business skills? His capacity in the business world?'

Margot twisted around to look at me. 'Anna,' she said, 'did you know about any of these business dealings?'

'No!' I spluttered. 'No idea! I had no idea that there was a business link between Babcia and Niles … you're saying they knew each other?' I just had to repeat this new fact. I was stunned and struggling to process this. My two worlds were linked? How could this be?

'Well, yes and no!' said Margot.

I hadn't wanted to look at Niles as I spoke, that would be too intimate. I just kept my eyes on Margot. 'But, you know … I'm not surprised to have been kept out of it,' I said. 'It's not like Niles ever shared anything about our finances with me.'

'But it was a family business. You're name's on it. Babcia said she had insisted on this from the outset.'

'Really? Why would Babcia have insisted on such a thing? I don't get it. I mean, Niles has to have control … of everything. But the thing is … our finances, the business … are out of control. They've been heading south for a while now. I know that much. And I only know this because Niles comes home and bitches about how it's everyone else's fault. He doesn't take any suggestions from me … no, no, no. It doesn't matter that I have background experience in my mum's family business or that I can see why our staff are so unhappy … No, I couldn't possibly have something to contribute. No, my role has always been just the person to blame. Somehow? I never know how. You know my mum warned me. She used to say to me, "He wants to dim your light to make him feel brighter".'

I'd gone on a tangent here, but I wanted to show Niles that I wasn't keeping our skeletons secret any longer. He was no longer going to intimidate me into silence. Hiding behind Margot, I had this courage. Is it courage if you're still hiding?

I'm sure Niles was reaching new levels of fury; he was being exposed, truly exposed. His private dealings were on the table, and the illusion of him being the successful businessman was shattered. He was being peeled away, layer by layer.

'I wouldn't be surprised if Detective Tarlington has you on his suspect list as Babcia's murderer,' Margot said. 'The question is why does a successful business-woman, a ruthless businesswoman at that, sink money into a failing business. Have you asked yourself this, Niles?'

Again, Niles seemed resolute to just hold his stare.

'Probably not,' remarked Margot. 'You're probably so entitled that you just think this money *should* come to you. It just should. You just put out your hand for this money. But why? Ask yourself.'

Niles was barely managing to compose himself at this point. 'You have this all wrong,' he said. 'The business has gone down because of interference from Babcia. You can never work with partners.'

'Actually, Niles, that is the version that you probably

tell the world, and yourself.' Margot was seamless in her quiet, unyielding tone. 'But it's just that … a version. A wonderful technique to deflect from reality and step away from your responsibility. Detective Tarlington, could you please elaborate on the facts here?'

Standing to attention, William then explained that Babcia was one hundred percent a silent partner. Niles had allowed her generous funds to evaporate through his own mismanagement. Babcia had no input whatsoever in his business decisions.

'But no,' concluded Margot, 'even you wouldn't be so stupid as to kill your benefactor.'

Niles was silenced.

Margot walked slowly to the right of the group. She had created a space between herself and William. Our eyes darted between them. Not knowing where to look. Was this to be a systematic roll call? I was sure that Margot was methodically working through information in her mind. I was sure I was not alone in wondering, *what's coming next?*

'Revenge is a very common motive for murder, is it not, Detective Sergeant Tarlington?'

'Absolutely,' he replied.

'Sometimes we can be so consumed by thoughts of revenge, we think our world will return to a more positive axis if the person who we feel has destroyed our world, isn't here anymore. Then we feel that they can no longer torment us.'

Margot glanced at William. 'We now turn to the discarded lover.'

'Babcia had a discarded lover?' I asked with quiet shock.

'I shall explain.'

Heads turned, one confused brow met another until Margot said, 'Tabitha, tell me about your brooch.'

'Margot, enough with your show; you're not impressing anyone. And now you want to talk about a brooch? Please!' Tabitha's patronising tone was lifelong practiced. She waved her hand away casually at Margot.

'Lily of the field,' Margot asserted.

With this, Tabitha sat upright to full attention. 'What?'

'What was the circumstance of your separation from your husband many years ago?' asked Margot.

'Sorry?' Tabitha was now almost hissing. I was sure she wanted to scurry away, a rare thing for this actress.

'It's well known, Tabitha, that you have lamented about your tragic love story high and low to probably everyone here and many more, I'm sure. Everyone, I noticed except for … Babcia?'

Tabitha said nothing. Her eyes narrowed.

'Let me remind you; we all know the tale. You were in love, but the man wasn't your husband. This lover was then almost kidnapped and trapped away from you against his will.'

'I don't see how that has anything to do with …'

'Yes? Have I got it so far?' The more agitated her target, the calmer Margot seemed to become. It was extraordinary to watch. Margot continued. 'His hideous wife didn't care for his happiness and snapped him right back to her. This left you distraught. Worse still, you had left your husband for your lover, and now your husband wouldn't take you back. You were left red-faced. That horrible wife of your lover devastated your world. Your life's unhappiness was all her fault. Am I close?'

'You can't think that I was talking about Babcia? Preposterous!' Although she held her chin in the air, her voice had lost its strength; it was fluttering.

'And worse still … he came from money … you envisaged an easy life … a luxurious life with him … and this too was taken away.'

This silenced Tabitha.

It was as if Margot was stalking her prey. 'Again, please tell me about your brooch?'

Tabitha withdrew. She instinctively drew her hand over her brooch.

'No? No explanation?' asked Margot. 'Okay, let me explain to everyone. Tabitha wears this particular brooch every time she comes to this gardening club. *Every time*,' Margot emphasised. 'Even when she's up to her elbows in dirt and wearing gardening clothes, the brooch is worn with pride.' All eyes were now locked on Tabitha. 'Why?' Margot took a moment. She didn't rush to satisfy her listeners. 'Suffice to say, seeing this peculiarity time and time again caught my attention. And as you know, Detective Tarlington, it is my way to research. I love a challenge. The delicate image on your brooch is called *Lily of the Field,* isn't it, Tabitha? And Detective Tarlington … shall I explain where this symbol and, in all probability, this brooch, originates from?'

Tabitha further scrunched the material beneath her brooch. She seemed as stunned as the rest of the group.

'Go ahead.' William did well giving the impression that he knew what was going on.

'The Slavic states. This is a classic Slavic symbol, a Polish symbol, and I'm sure that it had meaning to the person who gave it to you. This was a gift from your lover, wasn't it, Tabitha? I believe his name, Babcia's husband's name, was Tomek. And you've worn this brooch in an attempt to torment Babcia. You wanted to create doubt in Babcia; you wanted to provoke her, but it didn't work.'

'How do you …?' Tabitha whispered.

'As you somehow missed, Tabitha, Babcia had very poor vision up close. I realised this when I noticed that Babcia only criticised my garden from a distance. Up close, she wouldn't criticise my unimpressive plants; she could only criticise my flower's lack of smell. If she could have criticised me up close, she most definitely would have. She refused to wear glasses. Is that correct, Remy?'

'Yes … that's right. She was very stubborn on that point,' Remy replied.

'I'm sure she expected the rest of the world to adjust to her. All this time you would've felt delight in provoking Babcia, but I'm happy to say that she died without this torment.'

'Absolutely,' Remy said shaking his head. 'She definitely hadn't seen what was on your brooch. She never mentioned it. She definitely hadn't put this together. If she knew any this, I wouldn't have heard the end of it, and, Tabitha, you would have been kicked out of this club for sure.'

With this, Tabitha unleashed her vexation that had clearly festered over many years. 'She … she.' Tabitha struggled to speak. 'It wasn't his free will. He loved me. How could anyone love her? She ruined my life … and his! And then my poor darling, poor Tomek died. He died of a heart attack, but it was really a broken heart. He was a trapped animal, lost to cruelty. He died unloved, all because of that vulgar woman. I'm glad she's dead. You hear me! I'm glad she's dead.'

Remy put up a weary hand. He seemed tired by her, but he nevertheless asked, 'But how did Babcia not know who Tabitha was? How did Babcia have her at her Gardening Club and not realise? This is crazy … It makes no sense.'

I had been wondering the same thing.

'A valid question, but Remy, I think you know that

answer,' replied Margot. 'Babcia's way was often to shut out reality.'

'Yes … I've noticed that … It was her way. Her way of coping.'

'Exactly … probably something that she has needed to do since her childhood to be able to survive. This chapter, of her husband having a mistress, came up once in our time together here at the garden plots,' Margot said. 'True to form she told me that this hussy was not worth her time, that she never wanted to hear of her or see her, not even once. Also, for Babcia I think it wasn't really the done thing to speak of it. Babcia and Tomek would've forged forward with this being just another dark chapter that they put behind them … in a vault. They had suffered … struggling to make ends meet in war-torn Poland, immigrating to Australia, and the death of their only child … their son. Babcia would've found it undignified to talk of Tomek's *hussy* … her words. So simply, she refused to hear of and therefore to learn Tabitha's name. You might remember her saying tonight that *what mattered was that he was true in the end*. She alluded to this affair even tonight. No, Babcia would refuse to hear or speak of the *hussy's* name. She was below Babcia's attention.'

'Fascinating,' I said.

'She's always loved Tomek. Did you notice that she still wore her wedding band? She was devoted to him to the end.'

'No,' I said gently, surprised by Margot's error, 'that wasn't a wedding band. It was on her right hand, not her left.'

'Ha, good pick-up, Anna, but that was just Babcia being stubborn on a whole other level. In Poland, they wear their wedding rings on the right hand, not like here in Australia where we wear them on our left. This was Babcia holding true to her wedding vows and sticking to her European ways. Dedicated and stubborn.'

A strange and unpleasant sound came from Tabitha. Margot shifted to a more solemn tone, 'This affair chapter would've further chipped away at Babcia's ability to trust. From her childhood, she had learned not to trust. Her trust had now been violated by her own husband, her life partner, the person with whom she'd forged her escape from a previous life. This would've been devastating for her, and she'd have felt that he'd abandoned her. This is a sad theme from her childhood. She avoided getting close to people and being vulnerable with people by being like barbed wire.'

'Remarkable,' Remy said almost to himself.

Dean, Jacob and Niles were a silent audience, listening intently.

'You, Tabitha, came to the Narcissus Gardening Club out of a morbid curiosity to become familiar with Babcia, to meet your enemy. This, of course, is why you had your sights set on Remy. You prowled around him. Your daft attempts at making a play for

Remy were exaggerated even for you. You'd stolen one man from Babcia; now you wanted to steal another … Remy. Remy who was clearly a stabilising force for her. This would have been revenge for your lover returning to Babcia. You've been percolating your hatred. Your putrid detesting of Babcia has been all consuming for many, many years. You thought somehow this would give you release. Maybe you needed release from her. Maybe you needed her to not be here at all. Is this enough of a reason to kill, though? Is it? That's the question.'

William couldn't hide flickers of shock on his face. I wasn't even trying. My mouth was agape. This was a blindsiding revelation. How long has Margot sat on this knowledge, this piece of the puzzle? She observed and pulled at threads and then reconnected the story's tapestry.

I noticed William occasionally looking in the direction of the carpark. If a car did arrive, you would see the headlights shining in our direction through the layers of green. We were gambling with time. Margot was clearly going to get somewhere, but only if the police held off. I felt the urgency of our situation, but Margot somehow kept her even tempo. She was so measured in her manner, such a professional with her deep understanding of and ability to manoeuvre people. *Slow is smooth, and smooth is fast.* I'd heard these words from a military friend and they rang through my head. Margot was living this mantra. She looked like she was working through this with ease.

As swiftly as she began, Margot changed her attention to another potential candidate. 'What if Tabitha isn't the only person here consumed with toxic vengeful thoughts against Babcia? What if there is someone else who wanted nothing more than for Babcia to come to harm?'

And with this she turned her gaze on Dean. 'Your wife left you?'

'It's my turn is it? Sure, go your hardest.' Dean held his head high, his shoulders back, as broad as he could make them.

This would be interesting; Dean didn't need much to get angry. It looked like he planned to handle his way out of this.

'Isn't it strange that she suddenly left?' Margot continued unperturbed. 'Strange that she suddenly became quite strong and determined within herself. Don't you think that it's strange, Detective Sergeant Tarlington?'

'Yes … you could say that,' William said.

'Perhaps she might have started to think and act differently at a certain point? Did she, Dean? Some might say assertively; you might say otherwise?' Margot seemed to be intentionally pressing Dean's buttons; they were large and plenty.

'Are you saying that it's bad for a woman to speak her

own mind?' spat Dean. This was an impressive flipping of the conversation. A practiced skill, I dared say.

'Quite the contrary, I'm saying that this would've been particularly inconvenient for you.' Margot came to stand over him. This seemed to antagonise him beautifully. 'And what did you think when you found out that there was a reason, that there was a formidably strong woman who had stepped in as a support for your ex-wife? A woman who became her mentor, and guided her through, perhaps even gave her financial support to allow her to leave you since I'm sure you had control of the money. She gave your ex-wife choice, freedom, and she got her on her feet. I would confidently guess that this woman … Babcia, helped her with strong legal advice also.'

'Ludicrous. This is all conjecture. You're speaking nonsense, woman.'

'Well, *man!*' Margot shot back, 'we actually have evidence of Babcia's role, and you're the fool to have exposed it.'

'You're full of shit!' Dean was barely restraining himself.

William stepped forward. I saw a flicker of stress in his eyes. Poor William was watching his dear friend antagonising an explosion.

'Don't call a wolf out of the woods?' Margot said gingerly. 'You said this tonight. You said that your ex-wife used to say this to you many times.'

'What of it?' Dean smirked dismissively.

'You,' Margot continued with an incredulous look. 'You … the fool that you are, took yourself to be the wolf; you thought that you were the intimidator and took sick pride in this. But your ex-wife was actually saying, watch out because the strength in her was being awoken. Probably from protecting your children, hopefully from protecting herself. She was the wolf that was being called from the woods. You were tempting fate in your abuse of her. You were the one who exposed this to me … You exposed the fact that your ex-wife had learned Babcia talk. That Babcia was her guardian angel.'

'Would you stop calling her my ex-wife? We're still married; she's still my wife!' Dean snorted.

William really impressed me here. 'But are you together? Are you partners? Or ex-partners?' he said boldly.

'Exactly!' said Margot. 'If you're no longer together, most people use the title ex-wife or ex-husband. Most people respect and accept their ex-partner's choice to separate, Dean. Your ex-wife isn't a possession that you just get to keep. You don't have a claim over her if you don't have a current relationship.' I saw a flicker of a smile in her eyes. She was enjoying this.

She continued, '"Don't call a wolf out of the woods" is a classic Polish proverb, Babcia's language. This was Babcia's way of expressing her depth of meaning. So, with this foolish and misguided brag, you exposed to me that you were not in fact here for the joy of gardening … which is no surprise. You were here for Babcia!' Margot had built to a crescendo. She had a steel-like firmness as she eye-balled him. There was a sense of vindication here. I'd never seen Margot so impenetrable.

Margot switched to a mocking tone at this point, 'Dean, the truth is that you were here to prowl around the woman you believed ruined your life. In your mind, you're not responsible for why your ex-wife didn't want to be with you, why she needed to seek refuge. No! It is the person who provided a life raft for your ex-wife whom you blame, the woman who supported your ex-wife. That's like you bashing someone and then blaming the situation on the medics when they come to help.' Margot's word, *bashing*, was so strong, it jolted me. She wasn't wrong, but just so bold. Margot was definitely not backing down.

'There is no logic, no intelligence here,' she continued. 'Babcia would've played her role decidedly. She'd have been a formidable support and role model. Just what your ex-wife needed.'

Again, there was silence. I was sure, like me, everyone was absolutely intent on Margot. I'd completely forgotten the wilderness surrounding us.

To my astonishment, I then saw Remy stand to attention. 'Margot, Sergeant Tarlington, I have something I should probably show you.'

'Yes?' Margot frowned.

Remy reached into his pocket and handed William a small piece of folded white paper. I recognised it instantly. 'Dean dropped this earlier. Anna, she was there; she saw it too. I've been sitting on this, trying to work out if I was just wishing this to be evidence. Here, you decide.'

'It's a shopping list!' William waved the paper in the air, 'Remy, I don't ...'

'The writing, don't you recognise it?'

William now studied the note closely. 'The threatening letters to Babcia were all written in capital letters, sure, but look at the capitals there. They're written in cursive, and they look the same, you know,' Remy hesitated, 'the same as in the threatening letters to Babcia.'

'Why didn't you show this to me earlier?' William stepped toward Remy, the two tall men sharing eye contact that floated above the rest of us.

'Because I thought I was going crazy.'

'It's okay, Remy, it's okay.' Margot stepped in. She somehow didn't seem to consider the relevance of the note. 'Dean, you didn't kill Babcia.' Margot didn't skip a beat. She floored me.

'What?' Jacob gave a scoffing laugh.

'Dean's anger is the brutish, stupid type, don't you think Detective Sergeant Tarlington?' Margot just continued unperturbed.

'Hang on there!' Dean's face started to burn up, his eyes glared.

'Absolutely,' William seemed happy to jump in.

'While I'm sure that you're just as happy for Babcia to be dead, Dean, you're not controlled enough to plan this murder. And with your brute anger, you took pleasure in throwing bricks into Babcia's yard and writing threatening letters, fantasising about scaring her. As the coward that you are, you tried to be intimidating without actually turning up … without actually showing your face. Very juvenile of you.'

Margot, with an intentional look at William, said, 'Detective Tarlington, could you please tell us, how did Babcia respond to Dean's threats?'

William was happy to oblige. 'She was actually unfazed by it all. Given her background coming from a post-war country, this was nothing. She used many expressions to basically say it was a load of rubbish. It was Remy who was concerned for her safety, not Babcia. Babcia couldn't have given it another thought.'

'That pair of bitches.' Dean started shaking his head violently; I instinctively took even another step back. What seemed to tip him over was hearing that he hadn't unnerved Babcia. He hadn't caused the distress that he'd fantasised about. This was when he snapped. He was now opening up; the lid was off.

'Pair?' Margot asked.

'Yeah, the pair of bitches: my wife's aunty and

Babcia,' growled Dean.

'Your ex-wife's aunty?' Margot said as she stepped back. She had taken the pin out of the grenade and was now smart enough to stay out of the explosion range.

'Yeah, they were like those nosy neighbour types … spending too much time gossiping over the fence and meddling in everyone else's life. Throwing crap advice to people who are easy to manipulate and convince.'

'So, you're saying that your ex-wife met Babcia because Babcia was a neighbour of her aunty. Clearly your ex-wife's aunty was a support person for her, and once your ex-wife befriended Babcia, she also had Babcia in her corner.' Margot flung her hands open. 'And did I hear correctly that you found your ex-wife easy to manipulate?'

'Well, that's your narrative!' Dean bit back.

This stunned Margot briefly. 'That's your narrative? Where did you hear that psych pop talk? Do you actually know what that means? This isn't a narrative. We're collecting facts here, objective facts, not a subjective view!'

'Well, no, that's not what I said!' said a furious Dean.

'It sounds to me like you've lost your ability to manipulate your ex-wife. It sounds to me that you've lost control of her. And this Dean makes you … furious.' Margot's voice was strong and firm.

Dean looked like he was ready to launch at Margot. A savage in him had come out. Margot held his gaze unflinchingly. Staring at him from a physically safe distance with William at her side, she somehow calmly stated, 'I hope you didn't send the threatening messages and bricks to your ex-wife's aunt's house also?'

'Of course not, that would be traced straight back to me!'

'As this has now,' William interjected in his official voice.

Again, with abrupt decisiveness, Margot changed gear to another onlooker whom she found of course staring intently at her. Margot's momentum meant that you had no moment to gather yourself regarding the previous revelations. This was intentional, I was sure. It was like walking from one storm, directly to another. I felt completely disorientated, and that was just from my comfortable corner in the shadows. I couldn't imagine how it would feel if you were the centre of this. I would stay in my hiding place.

It was strange how Margot seemed to just shake off the intensity of Dean. Margot looked at Jacob. She sighed. William, Remy, Niles, Tabitha and I all followed her line of vision. We all looked with increasing curiosity at Jacob. The silence continued to sit untouched. I felt heat and chill both run through me.

'I'm not too worried about you Jacob,' Margot finally said.

Blank faces looked around. Jacob smirked awkwardly, his eyes quizzical.

'You're a stand-up guy; you've got an ailing wife who you look after. You say that she's pretty elderly and unwell, not long for this earth it seems, but you appear to be coping okay with all of this.'

Jacob looked back at Margot with a weary expression. 'Yep,' he said. A minimal word from the man who always had too much to say. Then he mustered up, 'Enough with the games, Margot. I'm getting very tired of all this. I'm glad that you're having fun at the expense of a lady who has just died. Have you forgotten? She was lying just a short distance away, straight up that arbour, and you stand there playing Cluedo.'

Had the ambulance, the police taken her away? Was she still lying there? What was the protocol here? My mind raced. Either way, William didn't correct him. Poor Babcia.

Margot just ignored Jacob's deflection.

'Little Jack Horner,' declared Margot with absolute bluntness.

'Sorry?' Jacob frowned.

'Do you recall the story of how Babcia had disowned her sister because she'd hooked up with a man who just wanted her for Babcia's wealth?' Margot then looked around at the group, indicating that this was in fact a question for the larger group. She received a procession of nods.

'To protect her sister,' Margot continued, 'Babcia arranged that her wealth would only go to her sister contingent on her separating from, I think I recall Babcia using the phrase, *the leech.*'

Walking further around the group toward William, Margot's voice was quiet and she looked at her feet. She gently rolled some stones underfoot. I had no idea what she was doing. 'Babcia of course, true to Babcia's way, refused to meet the *gold digger.* Babcia's sister was twenty years older than her soon-to-be husband and sadly, couldn't believe this was true of her fiancé whom she loved, so she didn't tell him before they got married. They married, and I imagine that upon discovering that the gold tap was turned off, her new husband would have been furious … utterly furious.'

She raised her head to again meet our unwavering eyes. 'Perhaps he became determined to find his way to the family money and spent the years plotting while his resentment grew. Formulating his plan, he'd just hang in there. Babcia had no other family for her money to go to after all.'

Heads started to turn to Jacob. Astonished questions crept into my mind.

Margot continued, 'But then he realised that if his wife was ill and died before Babcia, his plan wouldn't work; it would be a disaster. All of his work would be for nothing; Babcia had to die first. Babcia just had to die. He'd done his years, and it was his time to cash in. He'd found a way to watch Babcia, his rage fuelled his enjoyment of plotting her death. After he'd organised for Babcia to die, after he had murdered her, with no other family members alive, he'd then have his wife, her only surviving family member, contest Babcia's will, and he'd have all the wealth.'

I gasped.

'What?' Dean shouted.

'You?' Tabitha cried.

'For too long,' Margot barely paused, 'he'd had to pay his way and this wasn't what he signed up for. This wasn't what he was accustomed to. Then to make matters worse, he'd become his wife's carer. He couldn't mistreat her because it would be extremely easy for her to leave him. Babcia was like a rescue vessel waiting in the wings. A permanent encouragement for her if she ever made the decision to leave.' Margot paused. She stretched back her shoulders, then continued. Her eyes did not leave Jacob's. 'It was supposed to be easy street. It was "his money", and Babcia was his obstacle.'

From nowhere, the group heard Tabitha say, 'But Babcia's brother-in-law was Jack Horner. Babcia said that herself, many, many times.'

'A Little Jack Horner. This one is my favourite of Babcia's riddles. She tested me, I'll give her that.'

'A riddle? That's his name!' Tabitha corrected.

'Actually, Babcia was referring to his character … a type of person … a type of villain. She wouldn't say Jack Horner, she would say *A* Jack Horner.' Margot repeated this for emphasis, '*A Jack Horner.*' She paused, and we all hung onto her next words. 'This made the clue from the rhyme obvious to me and led me down the winding path of Babcia's logic. She was an extraordinary woman; so intelligent … a lateral thinker.' With that, Margot broke into rhyme. She spoke slowly, with rhythm and intention.

Little Jack Horner
Sat in the corner
Eating his Christmas pie
He put in his thumb
And pulled out a plum
And said, '*What a good boy am I.*'

'I think it's a pretty pertinent poem for her brother-in-law really,' Margot said smiling. She had a look of deep appreciation.

Tabitha was laughing. With a dismissive flicking of her hand, she said, 'Margot, you're crazy; you're actually crazy!'

Dean added in a patronising tone, 'But that poem is about eating … Margot, really?'

'It's about greed or gluttony,' I spoke up.

Margot, glanced momentarily at me, then continued calmly. She now started pacing around the room. Eyes followed her every movement. 'Exactly, Anna! Little Jack Horner didn't just want a piece of the pie, he wanted the whole pie, but it wasn't his pie to begin with.'

I watched, one, two, three frowns spread over the faces present. 'Historically, Little Jack Horner is about the act of opportunism and as you said Anna … it's about greed. But Little Jack Horner … it's not your pie; it never was your pie; get your thumb out, Jack; get your thumb out.' Margot now seemed to be speaking in riddles herself.

There was a general response of confusion.

'A thumb in a pie,' said Dean. 'Really!' The point was lost on him.

I was sure that Margot hadn't lost her way. William, however, began pacing. He had his hands clasped behind his back, hiding that he was constantly rubbing his thumb into his palm. 'This children's poem appears innocent, but it's not. As is the case with many traditional children's poems, it's actually pretty sinister. And this is what, or whom, Babcia was speaking of. In true Babcia style, she took poetic license in renaming her brother-in-law … a word play.'

Just as we had untangled the party lights earlier, Margot was untangling Babcia's life. She was the translator. 'Have you ever heard of a *Horner*?' Margot asked the group.

She received a wave of blank looks: Remy and Jacob stared directly at Margot, while Tabitha, Dean and Niles were alternating between their study of Margot and William. Perhaps they were looking for William's confidence in Margot to reassure them. I doubt anyone in the group thought they could keep up with Margot's solving of riddles. 'This refers to the playing of a trumpet during war time. There was a type of trumpet, a narrow-tubed instrument, and people who played them were called … *Horners*.' Again, she turned squarely to Jacob. 'I deduced Jacob, from your story of your wife, that your marital plight lined up with Babcia's story of her mysterious brother-in-law. You were a fool to share your marital story of woe with the group. But as is often the case when we're so busy feeling sorry for ourselves, we have little discernment, little self-control. As I said, in true Babcia style, she'd refused to meet her brother-in-law, so she wouldn't have recognised you. If you were the brother-in-law, then I expected your name to be linked to the name Jack Horner.'

'And Detective Tarlington, what did we discover was Jacob's surname? After all, we're all on first name basis here at the Gardening Club. Babcia didn't routinely know anyone's surname here; it was her hard-working personal assistant, Miss Idoia, who ran all the paperwork.'

William replied, 'Clarin, Jacob Clarin.'

Jacob was looking at the ground, but Margot just continued to bulldoze through. 'Jacob, a smart alternative of Jack, a derivative actually. I dare say that Jack is your real name? And Clarin? You couldn't change your last name as identification is required to get a garden plot here, but you could easily slip in a change to your preferred first name.'

Margot searched around the group with her eyes eventually resting again on Jacob. 'A Clarin is a type of horn instrument, is it not?'

Dean launched forward, his mouth agape. 'Shut the front gate!' he yelled.

With a cursory smile now to quiet Dean, Margot elaborated, 'You gambled when you came here using your real last name. You clearly didn't know the owner-ship … really … that Babcia had over the Narcissist Gardening Club. But you were in luck … that Babcia paid no heed to the actual running of the administra-tion; she left that to Ms Idoia. Babcia wouldn't have seen your surname on your application form; you were just Jacob to her. I'd got as far as learning what a Horner was. You see, the previous occasions that Babcia had shared this riddle with me had sparked my interest. "A Jack Horner". Fortunately, she gave me time to research, to try to think laterally, just like Babcia would. It was then that I'd researched the word *horner*. Some people play chess, others windsurf … I like to solve puzzles. And Babcia was a puzzle person's utopia. At the time this seemed like useless information … until tonight … I discovered your surname … Clarin … and there you go. It pays to follow your nose.'

'So Babcia didn't know who Jacob was?' asked

Tabitha, with childlike bewilderment across her face.

Jacob, or as we were now hearing Jack, bowed his head. He didn't disagree.

Margot continued with her momentum, 'You clearly came along as an experiment to see if you could slide in without drawing Babcia's attention. You succeeded.'

William worked very hard to hold his smirk. I knew this – finding anomalies and solving puzzles – was Margot's strength through and through. This wasn't work here for her; this was pleasure. She was just soothing her insatiable curiosity.

'We now know why your wife never came to these beautiful gardens.' Margot raised her eyebrows. 'She wasn't invited! I'm sure you barred her in fact. You of course could never let the two sisters meet. Their bond might have melted your wife's resolve to stay with you. She may have allowed herself to concede that she was wrong in her judgement of you.'

Jacob stood up and raised his chin to attention. He rolled his shoulders back and stood with determined sincerity. 'Okay, fine, yes, I'm the brother-in-law. I wanted to get to know this mysterious sister of my wife.' These words were spat with contempt. 'But that doesn't make me the murderer for goodness sake. I didn't murder the old duck!'

There was silence. Margot and Jacob eyeballed each other. No one moved. Jacob had reached for a chair beside him, stabilising himself. 'This doesn't mean that

I murdered Babcia,' he repeated. 'That's outrageous. I'm like Tabitha; I came here just to put a face to the villain in my life. Better the devil you know … all that.' Jacob turned with his back to us. He seemed determined to shut us all away from his gaze and his agitation.

Margot calmly replied, 'While I think Babcia was right, you are *A Little Jack Horner*, it's true there are no hard facts that point toward you being the murderer. We're just getting everyone's facts clear, and now yours are on the table.'

With this, you could see Jacob's body exhale.

Red and strained, Remy sprung to his feet, his towering form heaving with self-restraint. I was sure he was using every ounce of self-control not to launch at Jacob. But then with a snap, Remy twisted around and directed his anger at Margot; he just glared at her. I agreed in part with his anger, how could she just dismiss Jacob like that, after all that she'd unveiled. Dean and Tabitha were both still looking perplexed at Jacob, Tabitha's mouth blatantly ajar. William watched this pressure cooker bubbling; he was pensive, concentrating.

With all of this commotion and crossfire, I allowed myself to glance toward Niles. As soon as I realised that he was glaring at me, I looked away. We only held eye contact for a second, but there was something in his gaze that confused me. I hadn't seen the agitated

Niles; I had instead seen a look of curiosity from him. His expression lingered with me; it unnerved me. It was then that I realised that I was the only member of the group who had not been under Margot's microscope and the killer had not yet been unveiled. Niles was studying me. I couldn't help but feel it. I slowly turned my gaze to Margot. Surely Margot didn't suspect.

In Margot's abrupt way, she'd turned her attention from Jacob back to the group. 'Do you recall that there were three pieces of information that Babcia was able to share with the police? Firstly, the threats to her. Secondly, a business dealing. What was the third?'

The question was left hanging within the group's stifled shared atmosphere. 'The final piece of information was about a relationship!' Margot continued.

'What?' remarked Tabitha.

Margot pressed on, 'Babcia owned one of the largest storage businesses in the world; she was one of the wealthiest women in the country, not that you would know it from her worn shoes and sensible, weathered cardigan that she wore tirelessly. I recall …' Margot wafted off for a moment with warm sentiment, 'that she just loved that haggard cardigan. Her pockets with her treasures safely stowed.'

Margot's voice became louder, her words crisp and sharp. 'But what if her wealth doesn't go to her sister? What if her sister *isn't* her only surviving relative? What then?'

Jacob turned ever so slowly. He was at the back of the group. Perhaps I was the only one to notice that while he continued to gaze at the floor, he moved his head slightly to be in clear earshot of Margot's voice.

Margot continued, 'Babcia had a son.'

'Who died ...' said Remy firmly.

'Yes, who died,' conceded Margot, 'but before he died, what if he had a child?'

There was a wave of movement; we all leaned in toward Margot. 'Babcia informed William on their first meeting at her house that she and her son had been estranged during his last few years of life. Some of us have perhaps heard Babcia reciting this family tale?'

There were again several conceding nods acknowledging this piece of information. 'What she didn't tell us, but did tell the police, was that during this tragic family disconnect, her son had a child. A child that he didn't tell her about ... her grandchild. But Babcia had monitored her beloved son from afar. She had resources, and she used them well when something was important to her. This was crucial to her of course ... of utmost importance. From her sources, Babcia soon heard of this child and had the situation professionally investigated.'

Suddenly Margot turned to me. With her direct manner, she asked, 'Where did your parents meet?'

I felt the blood drain from my face. Everything went quiet ... I saw Margot talking, but for a moment

I couldn't hear her words. Her mouth was moving, but nothing. Everything started to spin; it was going black again. I saw Margot and William rushing to me. They were beckoning me to sit. I sat by Remy. I felt him come close to me and put a hand gently on my arm. I flinched. He withdrew. Why I flinched, I didn't know. Margot held me firmly. I clutched at the table in front of me; it became my anchor. I recovered. I breathed.

I don't know how much time passed. There had been silence. An outsider would've seen a group of people sitting in partial darkness frozen, just frozen. And then I whispered. 'They met on a research station, on a small research island off Tasmania.'

'Yes?' encouraged Margot.

She now moved in front of me and drew up a chair to the opposite side of my little table. She held my hands and drew her face close to mine. I could speak just to her now. I could concentrate just on her now. I was finding strength. 'The story goes that they only got together because they were stuck on this harsh but beautiful island … two people … one island … for months. As soon as they got off their research rotation, they went their separate ways. Mum told me that when she told him about the pregnancy, he was panicked. She told me that from the moment she found out that she was pregnant, however, the mother in her came alive … She was delighted to have her first, and as it turned out, only baby. They were both happy with the arrangement.

He went his way; we went ours. My mother told me that he generously provided for me. Mum never spoke ill of him.'

'No wonder Babcia was so confident about your paternity. An island! Is your father on your birth certificate?'

'Yes, but my father died when I was a teenager. I … I hadn't looked for him. I thought I would when I got older … but then … he died. I will never meet him. One of my biggest regrets.'

Margot said gently, 'Yes, your father died. And your grandmother has just passed away tonight also.'

I heard these words, but I couldn't digest them. With such kindness, Margot softly said to me, 'Now we know why she took the name Babcia … *Grandmother.* It was her most proud role. She thought of herself as a grandmother, your grandmother, even if it was from the theatre balcony seats. She was playing out this role in her mind.'

It was only after a little time that I became aware of the tears rolling down my face. I was transfixed on Margot's every word. I was trying to process all this but couldn't quite get there.

'Your father is Babcia's son. You are Babcia's grand-daughter,' Margot repeated more plainly.

I just sat there, fixating on Margot's face, on her words. I searched for understanding. I looked at her eyes, then her lips, then her eyes again, blue, red, blue.

I was trying to catch this information and hold it long enough to absorb it on any level. I needed to shake my state of shock; it wasn't helping me. I was needing to re-organise my whole life as I knew it. My world was expanding, yet contracting, in just a matter of seconds.

This state of overwhelm wasn't helped by Margot's next statement. She stood as if making a formal proclamation. 'And Anna …' She took some steps back. I waited. Then for some reason I stood also, to mirror her. 'You are the sole heir of her fortune. Her sister isn't her heir at all; you are. William has informed me that Babcia has an iron-clad will. Remy is to be paid his current wage for the term of his natural life. This is generous, but not a drop of money relative to Babcia's wealth. And her sister, Marigold, is to inherit a given amount every year that she's separated from her Jack Horner husband.'

'Bless her cotton little socks,' I heard Tabitha say.

There was no movement, not another word spoken; we were all transfixed by this unveiling of Babcia's world, my world. It was my story that completed the puzzle, a story that I'd never been told before.

Then, '*Bitch!*' Jacob roared.

I felt this motion coming at me. I saw a snapshot of Jacob. He had snatched up a mattock pickaxe. I saw the metal, the mass, the blade coming at me. He seemed to have lightning speed. I saw him bring it down on me. I didn't hear my scream.

I fell backwards. Freefall. No thought of falling. No bracing. All I could see, all I could think of, was the heavy, hurtling metal coming at speed to my face.

'*No!*' Remy shouted, lunging at Jacob.

William instantly followed.

There was a mash of bodies. Remy and William deflected his motion sideways. The three men landed on the concrete with a heavy thud, a dead-weight fall. Jacob landed amongst the scattered leaves with the two determined men pinning him down, the weapon propelled from his grasp.

Tabitha ran and grabbed the mattock away.

Splayed out on the ground, Jacob was yelling and thrashing hysterically. Enraged. Blood-curdling howls came from him. 'That little bitch … it's my money … years … years of planning … Finally, I get rid of the old bitch, and now this bitch is standing in my way. I've worked hard for it … I've waited … too long … too long. I haven't spent all these years only to be out done by a pathetic little bitch who thinks she can come here and take my money.' His eyes were grey, his face swollen, red.

At last, he collapsed with a bellow, 'All this, and she gets the money. That little bitch; that little bitch. It's my money. I promised myself I'd live and die a wealthy man.' He became unintelligent in his yelping. He sobbed.

'He's the spoiled little bitch!' barked Dean.

It wasn't till a moment afterwards that I noticed that Margot was by my side helping me up. I was lying on top of a pile of now-smashed terracotta pots. The second time that evening I'd found myself splayed out on the ground. My bruises tomorrow might make tonight seem more real.

CHAPTER VIII

Revelation upon revelation, what an extraordinary evening. At each turn I thought we had heard the worst of it, only to have to climb further through the complex human web. We all came to be on our feet again, utterly astonished by Jacob's explosive unravelling.

William instructed Dean to call on the police who were still securing the Birch Circle to attend. Jacob was swiftly handcuffed, all the while mumbling to himself. He was lost to this world. I at last succeeded in begging Margot, Remy and William to stop fussing over me. I understood their concern over the horror event that had just happened, but I was at the saturation point of numb. Somehow someone trying to kill me was, for now at least, just blending in with the theme of the evening. When you get hit by tsunami after tsunami, the size of the waves lose proportion. William phoned to update police headquarters; a conversation I would've loved to have overheard. With debriefing complete, Jacob was carted off. The relief on seeing his exit was immense.

Upon William's return, he seemed to breathe. He

looked to Margot, with an expression of deep gratitude and admiration and simply said, 'Thank you.'

A smile from Margot was all he received in return.

William, Margot, Remy and I stood in silence, taking in the moment. The party would soon be allowed to leave. We could now stand amongst the trees and begin to relax, to exhale from the night's tightrope. The gardens were returning from their previous enchanting quality. I could see beauty again. The smell of jasmine and citrus aromas soothed me, as we all took a moment to breathe, to quieten ourselves. The stars were now determined to be seen as they peered through into this small, private world of green. It seemed as if the previous commotion was somehow not real. The calm after the storm. Had it in fact happened?

Tabitha had wandered to another corner of the garden; she looked like a scarecrow, a silhouette in the darkness amongst the garden beds. A scarecrow figure with a cigarette in hand. Puff after puff, you could see the movement of the cigarette light in the soft darkness. It looked like a methodical firefly.

Margot could finally reach out and give her dear friend William an enormous hug. I saw tears in her eyes. Tears of shock, sadness or relief, I didn't know. She seemed to be coming down from the pressure of her daunting task. 'An evening to remember for all the wrong reasons,' she said.

Niles had removed himself to a far chair by the snow-pea trellis. He sat alone. I wasn't focussing on the money, but he would've been. He'd be ruminating on the fact that I was to be wealthy, and he was not. He would see this as power. I now had the means for immediate independence. Everything that was his currency, that he saw as leverage, I now had over him. He was smart enough to know, that from tonight, that I'd left him. He'd lost his power. What Niles didn't realise was that tonight's revelation actually had no impact on my decision to leave; that was already definite. Yes, the finances would grease the wheels, but the direction of my future was already set.

'You've done well. Yet again, I'm both proud and impressed,' William said as he gladly received Margot's hug, 'and horrified.'

'What a team, hey?' dismissed Margot, smiling at Remy and me.

'You were brutal,' said Remy.

Margot nodded slowly. 'I had no choice. I had to fly into the teeth of it.'

'You sure did that. You more than picked at a scab with these guys.'

'My plan was to rip the whole mess wide open.'

'Achieved,' William said grinning, 'and yet again, happy to be your wingman.'

'You're no wingman,' Margot said, laughing affectionately.

William exhaled; it was like he had held in his breath until now.

Margot said with eyebrows raised, 'Looks like you'll be able to present an open and shut case.'

'Absolutely,' said William. 'With Jacob, or Jack's confession heard by all, his link to Babcia and his attempt on poor Anna.' He nodded sadly to me. 'But you know … I should have realised Jacob's link to Babcia. He's her brother-in-law for goodness' sake. How did I not know that?'

'You were brand new on the case … and I doubt Babcia would have told you this story plainly, just riddles … You would have got there eventually. We just needed it to come out tonight.' Margot patted his arm lovingly. 'You'll have to downplay my role in all of this, if you don't mind, William. You can take the credit, and you take the paperwork. I think that's a fair deal.'

'You do hate paperwork,' William said, smiling broadly.

'Oh, I do.'

We continued to wander together in peaceful silence. I was relieved to finally have a moment when my brain was functioning again. I really had limped through the evening. 'I've just discovered and lost my family in the same night.' Interlinking my arm into his, I slowly whispered to Remy. 'So Babcia was my grandmother.' I'd need to say this many, many times to absorb it.

'And Babcia's sister, she's my great-aunty? I'll have to track her down, make sure that she's cared for, maybe connect?' It just dawned on me that she had lost her sister and in essence her husband. I imagined we'd be walking down this path together.

'I just wish she'd approached me earlier and told me who she was.' I wasn't saying this to anyone in particular. I knew that this would thrash around in my head for a long while yet.

'I hope you're not angry at me for not telling you,' said Remy, rubbing the stubble on his jaw, leaning down, looking intently for my reply.

'No way; you couldn't override her. It was her decision alone; you had to respect that.'

'No one could override Babcia,' Margot added.
I was perplexed by something Margot had said earlier. I was rallying; the anxiety I'd felt all night was melting away. 'What do you mean Babcia's been watching me?' I asked Margot. 'I chose to come to this garden club. I met her here.'

Margot cupped my face in her hands. 'Don't you see, my beautiful? You didn't win a prize of a garden plot; there was no prize to be won. These plots are fought over; you have to almost kill someone to get a garden plot here.'

Everyone looked with shock at Margot.

'Sorry,' Margot said. 'Anna, that gift was just sent to you under a creative ploy to have you come along. It was another one of Babcia's tests to see how you'd respond, if you would be grateful, which you were of course. Babcia couldn't tolerate those who just put their hand out. Did you know that you were one of the police's primary suspects for the death threats?' said Margot.

'What!' I said in astonishment. 'Me?'

William was nodding his head.

'Think about it. Babcia had extreme wealth, and you were her mysterious benefactor. They didn't have any other leads.'

'But I didn't know.'

'Beautiful … they didn't know that …'

Remy shook his head as he said. 'Yeah, that's another reason why Babcia didn't take the police involvement too well. It didn't get off to the best start you could say. She abused the police, tried to throw them out because they dared to suggest you were the culprit. She … well, you could imagine how that went down with Babcia.'

William looked up to take in the stars. 'Who would've thought.'

Margot smirked. 'Anyway, Babcia carefully choreographed it so that you would come along to the gardening club, Anna … She wanted to get to know you better before exposing your relationship. She's been watching you always though … since she heard of your birth.'

'All that time. My whole life!' This was a lot to take in.

'It took Babcia a long time to build trust. She needed to get to know you thoroughly first.'

I then heard Remy's soft words in my ear, 'She was planning to tell you. *Soon*, she'd say … *soon.*'

'And now this has been taken from you both.' Margot lowered her eyes to meet mine.

'Yes,' I said quietly.

Remy put his hand gently on my shoulder. This time I reached for him; I hugged him. Tonight we'd both had an enormous loss, his was loss of a relationship, mine was the loss of the relationship to come.

'I'll tell you anything you want to know about the whole story, the whole situation, about your grandmother, about your Babcia. I think I can help you get to know who Babcia was on a personal level. I think that … that might help you … if you like.'

'Wonderful … that would be wonderful.' Our precious hug was coming to an end.

'And Jacob! How about that!' exclaimed William.

Remy said with a philosophical air, 'There was a man who was so poor, so poor, all he had was money.' He looked intently to me. 'Jacob's heart is cold and hard; he'd be the poorest creature alive even if he did have Babcia's money.'

I was looking at Remy very closely. I was studying him. I felt like I was really looking at him perhaps for the first time. It was dawning on me more and more that while I knew very little about him, he knew so much about me, and this hidden world of mine. I actually felt okay about this; I felt safe.

'So Jacob.' William nudged Margot. 'He'd be the true narcissist at the Narcissist Gardening Club, yes?'

'No,' Margot said to our joint surprise. She shook her head. 'My dear William, how to explain. Take this daffodil here; let's have a chat about daffodils.'

William flicked his head to the side, squinching up his nose.' Well, I don't know anything about daffodils, Margot. I don't really care for them to be honest. I'm a lawn man myself, love a crisp mown lawn. Gardens aren't really for me. If it was up to me, I'd probably have complete lawn.'

'Well, that's a pitiful thought, but okay, let's talk lawn. There are different types of grasses, yes?'

'Yes.'

'Well just as there are different types of grasses, they're all lawn, there's different types or presentations of Narcissist Personality Disorder. You could say that it's an umbrella term for many expressions of this *type* of character. And here at the Narcissist Gardening Club my dear friend, we have a full array of expressions of narcissism, not just Jacob. As well as Jacob, we have Tabitha, Dean, and if you don't mind me saying, Anna, I think we could perhaps include Niles in this list.'

'Be my guest,' I said.

'We have ourselves a cluster. A very unfortunate but

not surprising cluster when we realise that they all had the same motivation, a classically narcissistic motivation, that of control, entitlement and a desire to cause emotional anguish.'

'And Niles, hey?' William said.

'Yes, I dare say that Niles is a Dean behind closed doors. Is that about right, Anna?'

'Absolutely,' I said without a thought needed.

'Street angel, home devil, hey?' said William lightly.

'So Babcia may have had her family's daffodil in mind,' Remy said, 'but she accidently named the Gardening Club quiet aptly.'

Cocking his head to the side, William looked perplexed. 'To think that Babcia was surrounded by sharks, and she never knew it. They were circling her, wishing her harm. Astonishing, all this, and she never knew.'

Margot considered. 'Imagine if Babcia knew all of this, all the back stories, all the vendettas coming at her. Her trust neuroses would be proven right ... she would have become even more untrusting of the world, if that's possible?'

'Well, ultimately, maybe Babcia was right?' I suggested.

'I don't know about that. Most of us have good hearts. We're human, and we screw up for sure, but our intentions are usually pretty good, and our conscience tortures most of us if we do harm to others. Most of us take responsibility for ourselves. Quite the opposite of these bad eggs.'

Remy considered. 'But the bad eggs, they cast the longest and darkest shadow, don't they.'

Margot had been quiet, down the rabbit hole of her own thoughts. In her beautiful, warm tone, she then said, 'I think Babcia was actually a sheep in wolf's clothing. The opposite of this lot!'

'She was like barbed wire to the world,' I said, 'because people leave barbed wire alone.'

'A sad truth,' William said. 'And what about the vodka?'

'Yes, the vodka!' Margot drew a breath. 'Do you recall that Babcia said *"that's ridiculous"* when Jacob said that Babcia had instructed him to bring the vodka?'

'Yes, I think so.'

'Babcia was many things, but she was also ruthlessly honest. When she said that she hadn't told Jacob to bring the vodka, that was true. He'd of course tried to make it look like it was her decision to bring it. Jacob knew that Babcia would embrace the vodka if he just brought it along, I mean he's married to a Pole. And indeed, Babcia was glad to be able to have a toast; this was an important event for her. She loved her gardening club, and she cherished the opportunity to have time with you, Anna. The vodka made the party a true event for her. And sadly,' Margot reflected, 'it was to be her last toast, her last *na zdrowie* as it were. You know the irony? With *na zdrowie* … we were toasting to good health … to longevity.'

'But wasn't the vodka going to be used in the punch we were making? Wouldn't this have ruined Jacob's plan?' William asked.

With this, Margot laughed. 'I must say … this is where Jacob … Jack … was very clever. Perhaps he knew from his Polish wife that Babcia hated mixing drinks … She considered mixing vodka as … as …' Margot searched for words, 'sacrilegious. She was a true Pol. All you needed to do was bring this up with Babcia and you'd get a lecture.'

'Sounds about right.' Remy was gently laughing.

'Jacob clearly knew this, and he also knew that making a toast was a big thing for Babcia … a cultural thing. All he had to do was suggest the vodka go in the punch and he knew she'd insist on shots after the setting up of the party. This was clever … I have to admit.'

'That's an ugly use of clever,' said William.

I think we each shared a strange reluctance to leave. Was I ready for the next leg, my next chapter? It would be immense; it would be exciting. For once I didn't feel scared. I'd spent the night feeling repelled; but now I didn't want the night to end.

Margot looked again to the stars. 'You know Remy, Anna … the Narcissus Gardening Club is now going to be free of Tabitha, Dean and obviously Jacob. We can claim it back. It can be a place where beautiful people come to enjoy beautiful things.'

'Are you going to change the name?' William asked us.

Margot didn't hesitate. 'Hell no, it's hilarious, and it's Babcia's legacy.'

'A Babciaism to the end!' I looked toward Remy. He put his arm around me. It felt good.

***